Anonymous

The Articles of Faith, and the Covenant

SALZWASSER
VERLAG

Anonymous

The Articles of Faith, and the Covenant

Reprint of the original, first published in 1859.

1st Edition 2022 | ISBN: 978-3-37512-386-4

Verlag (Publisher): Salzwasser Verlag GmbH, Zeilweg 44, 60439 Frankfurt, Deutschland
Vertretungsberechtigt (Authorized to represent): E. Roepke, Zeilweg 44, 60439 Frankfurt, Deutschland
Druck (Print): Books on Demand GmbH, In de Tarpen 42, 22848 Norderstedt, Deutschland

THE

ARTICLES OF FAITH,

AND THE

COVENANT,

OF

PARK STREET CHURCH,

BOSTON:

WITH A

LIST OF THE MEMBERS.

ALLEN AND FARNHAM, PRINTERS.

1859.

ARTICLES OF FAITH, AND COVENANT,

OF

PARK STREET CHURCH,

WITH A

LIST OF THE MEMBERS.

HISTORICAL SKETCH

OF

PARK STREET CHURCH.

EARLY in the year 1808, a little band of brethren of
the Old South Church in this city, moved by the low
estate of religion about them, the long absence of revivals, and the prevalence of doctrinal errors, formed
themselves into a Society for mutual religious improvement. In the summer of the same year, encouraged and
strengthened by the labors of the Rev. Dr. Kollock, of
Savannah, Georgia, then on a visit to Boston, they conceived the thought of building a new house of worship
and forming a new Church and Society on Evangelical
principles. Having received from Dr. Kollock an assurance that if they should carry their purpose into execution, he would become their pastor, a subscription was
immediately opened for the erection of a place for public
worship. In a short time, through great exertions and
sacrifices, they had $40,000 pledged for their work, and
on the evening of February 6, 1809, a meeting of the
subscribers was held to take the necessary steps in forming the new organization. A committee was appointed
to draw up ARTICLES OF FAITH, and a CHURCH COVE-
NANT ; to fix upon a lot of land ; and to procure the plan
of a building.

The Articles of Faith and the Church Covenant were
adopted February 23, 1809. On the 27th of the same

month, the Council to organize the Church met at the house of William Thurston, on Beacon Hill. The churches represented were : —

The Church in Charlestown, Rev. Dr. MORSE.

The Church in Cambridge, Rev. Dr. HOLMES.

The Church in Dorchester, Rev. Mr. CODMAN.

The exercises of the occasion were as follows : — Prayer by Rev. Dr. Morse ; the reading of the 4th chapter of the Acts of the Apostles, and discourse by Rev. Dr. Morse from Psalm cxviii. 25. The Articles of Faith and Government were read by the scribe, and signed in the presence of the Council by nine brethren and twelve sisters. They were then declared duly organized, and Rev. Mr. Codman presented to them the fellowship of the Churches. The same evening, before the Council dissolved, five members were added by profession to the new fraternity.

A call was immediately extended to Rev. Dr. Kollock to become their Pastor, and to Rev. Dr. Griffin, then professor elect at Andover, to officiate once on each Sabbath. Dr. Griffin at once accepted the invitation, though he did not commence his public labors with them till the completion of their house.

The corner-stone of the church edifice was laid on the 1st of May, 1809, with the following inscription : —

JESUS CHRIST
THE CHIEF CORNER-STONE :
IN WHOM
ALL THE BUILDING
FITLY FRAMED TOGETHER
GROWETH
UNTO AN HOLY TEMPLE
IN THE LORD.
THIS CHURCH FORMED
FEBRUARY 27TH,
AND THIS FOUNDATION LAID
MAY 1ST, 1809.

The ceremonies were conducted by Rev. Drs. Morse and Holmes. In September, Dr. Kollock declined their call, so great was the opposition to his removing from Savannah. Dr. Griffin was then invited to become their pastor, but declined. Many other calls were given and declined. In the mean time the house of worship was completed at a cost of over $70,000, and dedicated January 10, 1810. The sermon was preached by Dr. Griffin from 2 Chronicles vi. 18.

The call to Dr. Griffin was renewed February, 1, 1811, and accepted, and on the 31st of July he was installed. Dr. Griffin's ministry continued three years and nine months. He was succeeded by Rev. Sereno E. Dwight, who was ordained September 3, 1817, and dismissed April 10, 1826, after a ministry of eight years and five months. Rev. Edward Beecher was ordained as pastor in December of the same year, and exercised his ministry three years and ten months. After an interval of two years, Rev. Joel H. Linsley was installed December 5, 1832, and remained in office two years and ten months. After eighteen months, Rev. Silas Aiken was installed March 22, 1837, and dismissed July 12, 1848. Rev. Andrew L. Stone was installed January 25, 1849. The accessions to the Church from time to time, with the duration of the pastoral office in each case, are indicated in the table at the close of the list of members.

From the beginning, 1,952 members have subscribed the covenant of this Church, of whom 853 are now with us, 255 so far as our records show, have fallen asleep, and more than 800 have gone out from us to serve the cause of Christ in other walks of Christian labor.

The first general and powerful revival of religion in the history of this Church occurred in 1823, and added to its membership about 90 converts. Another outpouring of the Spirit followed in 1826–7, which resulted in

1 *

the addition to the Church of 100 members. In 1831-2, the Church was again largely blessed and increased. In the three years commencing with 1840, a powerful work of grace was enjoyed, which brought to the Church an accession of 250 members.

The connection of this Church with the movements of modern Christian benevolence is worthy of being held in grateful remembrance. The cause of Foreign Missions has been especially dear to it. The American Board, since its organization in 1810, has continued to receive the contributions of this Church. Some of the most efficient officers and members of the Board have been furnished by this Church. The Foreign Mission Society of Boston was formed in 1811, in the house of a member of this Church. The first foreign mission press furnished to the Board was projected by a member of this Church, and one fourth of its cost was given here. Since the formation of the American Board, about 180 of its missionaries have received in this house their parting instructions and farewell salutations. Here, on the 15th of October, 1819, a little band of seventeen were formed into a Mission Church to evangelize the Sandwich Islands, and the success of the enterprise is the brightest page of modern missions. For nearly fifty years there has existed in this Church a society of ladies to assist in clothing indigent pious young men while pursuing their studies for the ministry. The value of these contributions forms an aggregate of more than $10,000. In 1826, a movement was set on foot by a member of this Church, who devoted his life to the work, to improve our system of prison discipline, and ameliorate the condition of the convicts of the land. In the same year an idea was suggested and discussed at the house of one of the members of this Church, which led soon after to the formation in the city of New York of the American Home Missionary

Society. The agency exerted by this Church in estab-
lishing in its present form the Monthly Concert of Prayer
for the conversion of the world, in commending to general
observance the annual concert of prayer for the Colleges
of the land, in promoting the organization of the American Temperance Society, and the American Education
Society, are matters in its history worthy of grateful com-
memoration. In view of such a record the Church may
well exclaim, " Ebenezer," — " Hitherto hath the Lord
helped us."

PASTORS.

Rev. EDWARD D. GRIFFIN, inst. July 31, 1811, dismissed April 17, 1815.
Rev. SERENO E. DWIGHT, ord. Sept. 3, 1817, dismissed April 10, 1826.
Rev. EDWARD BEECHER, ord. Dec. 27, 1826, dismissed Oct. 28, 1830.
Rev. JOEL H. LINSLEY, inst. Dec. 5, 1832, dismissed Sept. 28, 1835.
Rev. SILAS AIKEN, installed March 22, 1837, dismissed July 12, 1848.
Rev. ANDREW L. STONE, installed January 25, 1849.

DEACONS.

JOHN E. TYLER, chosen December 8, 1809, died January 26, 1821.
JOSIAH BUMSTEAD, chosen December 8, 1809.
JEREMIAH EVARTS, chosen May 4, 1819, died May 10, 1831.
JOHN C. PROCTOR, chosen May 4, 1819, resigned August 24, 1827.
HENRY HILL, chosen March 2, 1825, resigned April 21, 1837.
NATHANIEL WILLIS, chosen September 19, 1827, resigned Sept. 3, 1847.
NATHANIEL DANA, chosen May 14, 1835, resigned February 5, 1847.
DANIEL SAFFORD, chosen June 14, 1837, resigned May 27, 1842.
EDWIN LAMSON, chosen July 12, 1842.
GEORGE RUSSELL, chosen March 10, 1847, died March, 1857.
HENRY HOYT, chosen April 28, 1847.
EZRA FARNSWORTH, chosen December 14, 1853.
TYLER BATCHELER, chosen September 17, 1857.
JACOB FULLARTON, Jr., chosen October 13, 1857.
CHARLES C. LITCHFIELD, chosen October 13, 1857.

RULES AND REGULATIONS.

1. The weekly prayer meetings of the Church shall be held on Friday evenings; and every such meeting shall be considered a regular Church meeting for the transaction of business.

2. The annual meeting of the Church for devotional exercises shall be held on the last Friday evening of February, except when that interferes with the preparatory lecture, in which case it shall be on the following Friday evening.

3. The annual business meeting of the Church shall be on the last Monday evening of February.

4. The sacrament of the Lord's supper shall be observed once in two months, namely, on the 1st Sabbath of January, March, May, July, September, and November, after the public services of the afternoon.

5. The preparatory lecture shall be on the preceding Friday evening.

6. The Examining Committee shall satisfy themselves of the proper qualifications of all candidates *coming either with or without certificates.*

7. Persons approved by the Committee shall be announced to the Church on Friday evening three weeks before the preparatory lecture, at which time all certificates shall be read.

8. They who are to be received from the world shall be propounded before the congregation on the second Sabbath preceding the sacrament.

9. On the evening of the preparatory lecture the Church shall be led to a vote on the question of receiving the candidates, on condition that they shall afterwards subscribe the articles of the Church, and if they have not brought

certificates, give their public assent to the covenant. The vote shall be taken on each case separately.

10. On the Sacramental Sabbath before the administration of the ordinance, the covenant shall be read in the presence of the congregation to those who are to be received from the world, to which they shall signify their assent. At the same time, the minister shall declare publicly that A, B, and C have been received by certificate from other churches, naming the churches particularly.

11. A general invitation shall be given from the pulpit previous to the Sacrament, to all members of evangelical churches present, in regular standing and full communion, to partake of the ordinance.

12. All members absenting themselves from the worship and communion of this Church for one year or more, shall satisfy the Committee in respect to their reasons for so doing, or apply for a letter to some other church.

13. All requests for letters of dismission and recommendation shall be read at the church meeting on Friday evening, and referred to the Examining Committee, and on the next succeeding Friday evening shall be acted on by the Church. Such letters shall be considered valid one year only from their date.

14. The chairmen of committees on collections shall present in each case written reports of the sums collected, which shall be placed on the files of the Church.

15. The Clerk of the Church shall present a report, at the annual devotional meeting of the Church, of the amount of collections for benevolent purposes during the year.

16. Members of other churches having communed with this Church for the space of one year, will be required at the expiration of that time to apply for admission, or assign to the pastor a satisfactory reason for not doing so.

17. Every candidate for the pastoral office in this Church, shall be required, prior to his installation, to subscribe to the Articles of Faith adopted by the Church, and as soon thereafter as convenient become a member of the Church.

The following table presents a list of the benevolent causes to which the Church regularly contributes, and the time of their annual presentation.

JANUARY,	Foreign Missions.
FEBRUARY,	Education Society.
MARCH,	American and Foreign Christian Union.
APRIL,	City Missions.
MAY,	Bible Society.
JUNE,	Western College Society.
JULY,	Sabbath Schools.
SEPTEMBER,	Seamen's Friend Society.
OCTOBER,	Home Missions.
NOVEMBER,	Tract Society.
DECEMBER,	Church charities.

ARTICLES OF FAITH AND GOVERNMENT.

Adopted February 23, 1809.

WE, the Subscribers, having agreed to unite in the establishment of a new Congregational Church in Boston, by the name of *Park Street Church*, think it proper to make a declaration of that Faith which is the bond of our ecclesiastical union, and which we shall expect to find in all those who shall hereafter participate in our religious privileges and communion.

First. We believe that the Scriptures of the Old and New Testament are the Word of GOD, and the only perfect rule of Christian faith and practice.

Second. We profess our decided attachment to that system of the Christian religion which is distinguishingly denominated *Evangelical*; more particularly to those doctrines, which in a proper sense, are styled the Doctrines of Grace, namely: " That there is one and but one living and true GOD, subsisting in three persons, the FATHER, the SON, and the HOLY

GHOST; and that these Three are the one GOD, the same in substance, equal in power and glory; that GOD from all eternity, according to the counsel of His own will, and for His own glory, foreordained whatsoever comes to pass; that GOD in His most holy, wise, and powerful providence preserves and governs all his creatures and all their actions; that by the Fall, all mankind lost communion with GOD, are under His wrath and curse, and liable to all the miseries of this life, to death itself, and to the pains of hell forever; that GOD, out of His mere good pleasure, and from all eternity elected some to everlasting life, entered into a covenant of grace, to deliver them from a state of sin and misery, and introduce them into a state of salvation by a Redeemer; that this Redeemer is the Lord JESUS CHRIST, the eternal Son of GOD, who became man, and continues to be GOD and man in two distinct natures and one person forever; that the effectual calling of sinners is the work of GOD's Spirit; that their justification is only for the sake of CHRIST's righteousness by faith." And though we deem no man or body of men infallible, yet we believe that those divines that were eminently distinguished in the time of the Reformation, possessed the spirit, and maintained in great purity the peculiar doctrines, of our holy religion; and that these doctrines are in general, clearly and happily expressed in the Westminster Assembly's Shorter Catechism, and in the Confession of Faith owned and consented unto by the Elders and Messengers of the Churches, assembled at Boston (N. E.), May 12th, A. D. 1680.

Third. In regard to our ecclesiastical government and discipline, with our sister churches in this Commonwealth we adopt the Congregational form, as contained in the Platform of Church Discipline, gathered out of the Word of God, and agreed upon by the Elders and Messengers of the Churches, assembled in the Synod at Cambridge (N. E.), A. D. 1648.

Fourth. In order to admission to membership in this Church, it is understood that every Candidate shall be previously examined, and give credible evidence of a ground of the comfortable hope of a personal condition of grace, through the renovation of the soul, by the special influences of the HOLY SPIRIT, implying repentance for sin and faith in JESUS CHRIST the Redeemer.

Finally. We hereby covenant and engage, as fellow Christians of one faith, and partakers of the same hope and joy, to give up ourselves unto the Lord, for the observing the ordinances of CHRIST together in the same society, and to unite together into one body for the public worship of God, and the mutual edification one of another in the fellowship of the Lord Jesus; exhorting, reproving, comforting, and watching over each other, for mutual edification; — looking for that blessed hope and the glorious appearing of the great GOD, even our Saviour JESUS CHRIST, who gave Himself for us that He might redeem us from all iniquity, and purify unto Himself a peculiar people zealous of good works.

FORM OF ADMISSION.

ADDRESS.

You have presented yourselves in this public manner before God, to dedicate yourselves to His service, and to incorporate yourselves with His visible people. You are about to profess supreme love to Him, sincere contrition for all your sins, and faith unfeigned in the Lord Jesus Christ: to enter into a solemn covenant to receive the Father, Son, and Holy Ghost, as they are offered in the Gospel, and to walk in all the commandments and ordinances of the Lord blameless. We trust you have well considered the nature of these professions and engagements. The transaction is solemn, and will be attended with eternal consequences. God and holy angels are witnesses. Your vows will be recorded in heaven, to be exhibited on your

(15)

trial at the Last Day. Yet be not over-whelmed. In the name of CHRIST you may come boldly to the GOD of grace, and provid-ed only you have sincere desires to be His, may venture thus unalterably to commit yourselves, and trust in Him for strength to perform your vows.

Attend now to the

COVENANT.

In the presence of GOD, His holy angels, and this assembly, you do now solemnly dedi-cate yourselves to GOD the FATHER as your chief good; to the SON of GOD as your Mediator and Head, humbly relying on Him as your Prophet, Priest, and King; and to the HOLY SPIRIT as your Sanctifier, Comforter, and Guide. To this one GOD, FATHER, SON, and HOLY GHOST, you do heartily give up yourselves in an everlasting covenant to love and obey Him.

Having subscribed the *Articles of Faith and Government* adopted by this Church, you promise to walk with us in conformity to them, in submission to all the orders of the Gospel, and in attendance on all its ordinances, and that, by the aid of the Divine Spirit, you will adorn your profession by a holy and blameless life.

This, you severally profess and engage.

[If the candidate have not been baptized, the Ordinance of Baptism is to be here administered.]

In consequence of these professions and promises, we affectionately receive you as members of this Church, and in the name of CHRIST declare you entitled to all its visible privileges. We welcome you to this fellowship with us in the blessings of the Gospel, and on our part engage to watch over you, and seek your edification, as long as you shall continue among us. Should you have occasion to remove, it will be your duty to seek, and ours to grant, a recommendation to another church; for hereafter you can never withdraw from the watch and communion of the saints, without a breach of covenant.

And now, beloved in the Lord, let it be impressed on your minds, that you have entered into solemn circumstances from which you can never escape. Wherever you go, these vows will be upon you. They will follow you to the bar of God, and in whatever world you may be fixed, will abide upon you to eternity. You can never again be as you have been. You have unalterably committed yourselves, and henceforth you *must* be the servants of God. Hereafter the eyes of the world will be upon you; and as you demean yourselves, so religion will be honored or disgraced. If you walk worthy of your profession, you will be a credit and a comfort to us; but if it be otherwise, you will be to us a grief of heart and a vexation. And if there is a wo pronounced on him who offends *one* of Christ's little ones, wo, wo to the person who offends *a whole Church!* "But beloved, we are persuaded better things of you, and things that accompany salvation, though we thus speak." May the Lord guide and preserve you till death, and at last receive you and us to that blessed world where our love and joy shall be forever perfect. Amen.

MEMBERS

OF

PARK STREET CHURCH, BOSTON.

Those with *t* preceding the name were received by transfer from other churches; the others were received on the profession of their faith. The letter succeeding the name, shows how the connection was dissolved; *t*, by transfer, *e*, by excommunication; *d*, by death.

February 27, 1809.

t William Thurston *d* 1822
t Elizabeth Thurston *t* 1822
t John E. Tyler *d* 1821
t Hannah B. Tyler *t* 1826
t Caleb Bingham *d* 1817
t Hannah Bingham *d* 1820
t Josiah Bumstead
t Mary G. Bumstead
t William Ladd *t* 1828
t Mary Ladd *t* 1828
t Daniel Baxter *d* 1838
t Sarah Baxter *d*
t Joseph W. Jenkins
t Abigail Jenkins
t Andrew Colhoun *t* 1842
t Martha Colhoun *d* 1831
t John Holbrook *d*
　Henry Homes *d* 1845
　Aaron Hardy *d* 1816
　Ebenezer Parker *t* 1830
　Asa Ward *t* 1847
　George J. Homer *d* 1845
t Hannah Haskins *d* 1819
t Elizabeth Haskins *d*
t Fanny Haskins *d*
t Mary Turner *d* 1838

March 2, 1810.

t Mary Perry *t* 1822
t Elnathan Duren *e* 1828
t Dorcas Homes *d* 1813
t Lucy Ingalls *d* 1823
t Daniel Beal *t* 1813
t Mary Beal *t* 1813

March 26, 1810.

t Jonathan Kilton *d* 1816
t Margaret Kilton *d*

April 8, 1810.

t Susanna Freeman *d* 1832

April 22, 1810.

Elizabeth Devens (Gallep) *d*
Samuel Train *t* 1831

April 24, 1810.

t Benjamin Scott *d* 1825

March 2, 1811.

t Daniel Grover *d* 1847
t Isaac Reed *t* 1814
　Abigail Scott *d*
　Mary Ingraham (Russell) *d* 1834

Sarah Cheesman (Cushing) *t* 1841
t Nancy Cushing *t* 1820

[Rev. E. D. Griffin, D. D., installed July 31, 1811.]

August 30, 1811.

Henrietta Hopkins *d* 1816
Eleanor Kettell *d* 1839
t Margaret Aiken *d.* 1815.
t Benjamin Beckford *t* 1831
t Margaret Beckford (Kneeland) *t* 1836
Elizabeth G. Furber *d* 1824
Robert Cunningham *d* 1823
t Ann Freeland *d* 1814
t William W. Lamson *e* 1814

November 29, 1811.

Asenath Read (Parsons) *t* 1829
t Nancy Smith *t* 1814
t Deliverance Adams *d* 1813
t Kezia Adams (Jones) *d* 1839

February 28, 1812.

Maria V. Ball *d* 1826
Sarah Huly *t* 1822
Amasa Fisk *e* 1813
Mary Fisk *d* 1829
Rebecca Ann Morse *t* 1817
Nabby Cary *e* 1828
t Hannah Parker *d*
Mary Richardson *e* 1816

June 5, 1812.

Elizabeth Greenwood (Hovey)
t Hannah Spofford *d* 1833
t Margaret Cooper *d*
t Mehitable Chadwick *t* 1825
Pamelia Hollis *d*
t Elizabeth Harlow *t* 1825
t Silas Barrett *t* 1820
Joseph Morton *t* 1819
Elias Maynard *t* 1821
Joanna Maynard *t* 1821
t Elizabeth Duren *t* 1815
t Deborah Weston

September 4, 1812.

Silence Hayden *t*
Eudoxa Nickerson *d* 1834

Margaret Shipley *e* 1828
Betsey Nichols *d*
t Naamah Farrington *t* 1827

December 4, 1812.

Joshua Coburn
Eunice Coburn
Anna Pratt *t* 1815
Bathsheba Thomson *d*
James Steel, Jr. *d* 1814
t Abigail Kidder *d*
Clarissa Harlow *t* 1825
t Eunice Beckford (Hunt) *t* 1831

March 5, 1813.

t Nathaniel Willis *t* 1847
t Hannah Willis *d* 1844
Catharine Lamson *d* 1829

June 4, 1813.

t Francis Brown *d* 1826
t Sarah Withington (Vose)
Thomas L. Paine *t*
Luke Coburn *d* 1816

September 3, 1813.

Priscilla Karson *t* 1828
Priscilla Kilham
John D. Furber *d* 1840
Charles Keith *t* 1815
Sybil Keith *t* 1815
Ezra Palmer *t* 1825
Elizabeth Palmer *d* 1822
Dolly Everett *t* 1827
Nancy Emerson *t* 1814
Harriet Gridley *t* 1818
Ephraim Wetherbee *d* 1819

December 3, 1813.

t Sally Sturtevant (Cushman)
Simeon Palmer *d* 1853
Hannah Stoddard *t* 1824

March 4, 1814.

t Mary Brown *t* 1816
t Lewis Davenport *d* 1821
Rhoda Jones *d* 1830
t Elizabeth Dempesy *e* 1829
t Sarah Soren *d*
t Sally J. Soren *t*
t Ruth Denton *t* 1817
Phebe Harlow *t* 1825

t Sylvanus Baldwin *t* 1817
t Nabby Baldwin *t* 1817
Elisha Bass *t* 1826
William Kehr *t* 1819

December 2, 1814.

t William Bates *t* 1835
t Gardner Tufts *t* 1824
t John H. Munroe *e* 1817
t Hannah Munroe *d* 1819
t Elizabeth Harlow *t* 1825
t Mary Hosley (Hammond)

March 3, 1815.

William Adams *t* 1827
Elizabeth M. Tyler *d* 1819
Mary Winn *t* 1819
Anna Briant *t* 1824
Betsey C. Parkhurst (Adams) *t* 1827
t Richard Pearse *d*
t Danah H. Pearse *d*
Josiah Coburn *t* 1825

[Dr. Griffin dismissed April 27, 1815.]

May, 1815.

Mary Lee Kimball (Gurney) *t* 1815
William Kidder *t* 1817
t Mercy Delano *d*
Sally Adams *d*
Sarah Ashton (Safford) *t* 1827
Eliza Holmes (Dickinson) *t* 1847
t Daniel Safford *t* 1827
John W. Rogers *t* 1822
Benaiah Briant *d* 1819
Sarah Coburn *t* 1825

September, 1815.

t John Cleaveland Proctor *t* 1827
Elizabeth Lakeman *e* 1820
t Nancy Holmes *d*

November 26, 1815.

Henry Wenzel *d* 1824

March 3, 1816.

Sarah Parker *d* 1821
Polly Moore *d* 1849

Mary Wright *t* 1839
Martha Rogers *t* 1822
Mary Chipman (Paine) *t*

June 2, 1846. 1816

Olivia Woodman (Bacon) *t* 1830
t Isabella Homes

August 25, 1816.

t Rhoda Ware *d*
t Lydia Ingalls *d*
t Sally Wilson *d* 1824
t Daniel Gregg *d* 1849

November 30, 1816.

t David Hale, jr. *t* 1822
t Laura Hale *t* 1822
Martha Atkins Quincy
Margaret Crawley (Tufts) *t* 1824
t Hannah Furber *d* 1822

February 23, 1817.

Harriet Maynard *d* 1821
Eunice Nickerson (Whiting) *t* 1827
Salome Nickerson (Hinckley) *t* 1843
Mary Nickerson *t* 1829
Marcus Whiting *t* 1827
Charles J. Hadley *e* 1833
Sarah Kimball *t* 1827
Sarah Ladd *t* 1823
Andrew Ellison *t* 1849
Mary Ellison *d* 1832

May 31, 1817.

t Isaac J. Moors
Naamah Moors
Ruth Thomas Cushing (Dill) *t* 1830

August 31, 1817.

t Sereno E. Dwight *d*

[Rev. Sereno E. Dwight ordained Sept. 3, 1817.]

September 5, 1817.

Sarah Morton
Mary C. Smith *t* 1820
Elizabeth B. Ingalls *t* 1836

December, 1817.

t Lucia G. Swett *d* 1844
t Nancy Proctor *t* 1827
t Louisa Battelle (Foot) *t* 1826
t Jeremiah Evarts *d* 1831
t Sophia Munroe
·*t* Abigail B. Quincy *d* 1834
Jonathan F. Greenwood *d* 1826
t Mehitable Evarts *d* 1851
t Betsey Searles *t* 1820

March 1, 1818.

t John Fairbanks *d* 1823
Charlotte Vose *t* 1844
Lucy French (Wenzell) *d* 1833
t Sarah Gamage *t* 1843
t Thomas M'Clure *d* 1826
t Mary M'Clure *d* 1831
Sally Everett *t* 1828
t Jechonias Thayer *t* 1830
t Eliza Thayer *d* 1817
t Ezra Haskell *t* 1822
t Joanna Lord *t* 1834
Sophia Lapham (Dunbar)

June 7, 1818.

Samuel C. Lee *t* 1824
Ebenezer Nickerson *d*
Almira Goddard *t*
Mary Ladd *t* 1824
t Willard Williams *t* 1822
t Martha W. Bliss
Abigail Hapgood (Gilman) *t* 1829
t Sylvia T. Nutting (Buyn) *t* 1832
t Sally Trumbull *t* 1831

September 6, 1818.

Levi Chamberlain *t* 1822
t Elizabeth Eaton *t* 1835
Sarah Powers *t* 1842
Martha H. Gray (Bancroft) *t* 1825
Asa B. Hogins *e* 1833

December 8, 1818.

t Eunice Hale *t* 1822
t Lydia Peabody *t* 1844
Sarah Jane Wiggin *t* 1822
Isaac Davis, Jr. *t* 1832
Polly Davis *t* 1832

t Betsy Witham (Bingham) *t* 1837
t Hannah Tileston *d* 1829
Eliza Edes *t* 1826
Margaret Johnson *t* 1855
Lucy Jenkins (Libby) *t* 1827
t Anna Hewins
Abner H. Hardy *t* 1820
Asenath Hardy *t* 1820

March 7, 1819.

Eliza Nash *t* 1840
Eliza G. Homer *d* 1822
Candace Spear (Horton) *t* 1847

June 6, 1819.

Elizabeth Ludden *d*
Jairus Pratt *t* 1824
t Ellen Stetson (Arkansas Mis.)
t Joseph B. Smith, Jr.
t Sally W. Smith

September, 1819.

H. R. French *t* 1826
t Mary Newell *d*

November 7, 1819.

Frances Crane *t* 1828

December, 1819.

t Sally Jewett *t* 1830
t Rebecca Langdon *d* 1821

March, 1820.

Roxana Smead (Thayer) *t* 1847
Elizabeth Grover *d* 1821

April, 1820.

Dorcas Gemmil
Mary I. Beckford (Dickinson) *t* 1826
Josiah H. Vose *t* 1844
T. Winnifred Atkins
Elizabeth D. Gray (Willey)

June, 1820.

Amos Hunting *d* 1832
John Adams Vinton *t* 1829
Esther Bradlee *d* 1824
Ruth Caryl *d* 1847
Rebecker Souther *t* 1841
Catharine Weatherwax *e* 1829

Harriet Weare *t* 1834
t Laura Tileston *d*
Ann E. Day *t* 1827
Susan Day (Johnson) *t* 1827
Mary Gould *d* 1825
Mary Soren (Haskins) *t* 1827
Martha Soren (Hartford) *t* 1839
t Rachel Abbot *d*

September 3, 1820.

Hannah Eliza Clark
John Gammell, Jr. *t* 1827
Caroline Johnson
Lydia Johnson (Jones)
t Harriet Edson *t* 1831
t Hannah Duren *t* 1831
t Lucy Gillpatrick *t* 1827

December 3, 1820.

Belinda Cross (Pierce) *t* 1826
Cynthia Dixey (Clark) *t* 1828
Nathan Johnson *t* 1827

March 4, 1821.

Nathan Barrett *t* 1827
t Nancy Dickinson *t* 1826
Ann Williams (Bundy)
Ruth Gould *d* 1831
Joseph W. Edson *t* 1831
t Hannah Farrar *t* 1825
Abiah F. Homer (Cobb) *t* 1848
t Beulah Wilder *t* 1826
t Peter Meston *t* 1825
Samuel Hubbard *d* 1847

May 28, 1821.

Frances Bancroft *d* 1821
t Elizabeth Simpson *t* 1829
Angelina Sanborn (James) *t* 1836
Jesse W. Morse *d* 1830
t Lucy C. Morse *t* 1832
John Bennett *t* 1825
t Eunice B. Whitney (Clark) *t* 1831
Isaiah Souther *d* 1837
Susan Adams *d*
Margaret K. Skinner (Weatherston) *d*

* *September* 2, 1821.

t Betsy Stevens *t* 1827

Nathan Tyler *t* 1828
Abner Chapman *d*
Andrew Bradshaw *t* 1822
Isaac H. Parker *t* 1825
t Ebenezer Hayward *t* 1828
t Sarah Hayward *t* 1828
t Lucy Proctor *t* 1828
William G. Lambert *t* 1825
Daniel Noyes *t* 1822
Benjamin Bennett *t* 1844
t Dexter Gilbert *t* 1827
Gilman Prichard *t* 1822
t Benjamin Kingsbury *t* 1827
Betsey Hobart *t* 1835
Aaron Woodman *t* 1822
John Dane *t* 1844
Isabel Meston *t* 1825
Frances Porter (Wheeler) *d* 1832
t Mehitable S. Hart *c* 1825
t Esther Melcher *d*
t Aaron H. Patten *t* 1826
t Sally Newhall

December 2, 1821.

Lucy D. Willis (Bumstead) *t* 1827
Mary B. Scott *d* 1826
Ruthy Clark *t* 1831
t Sarah C. Moore *d*
George Odiorne *d* 1847
t John Benson *t* 1835
t Clara M. Benson (Thurston) *t* 1840

March 3, 1822.

t Hannah Grozer *t* 1834
Hannah S. B. Prince *t* 1833
Thrypena S. Clapp *t* 1827
t Nancy Hawkins *t* 1844
Martha V. Chickering (Hooker) *t* 1827
Isaac Clark
Joseph Jenkins *e* 1841
t Martha Vinall *t* 1838

June 2, 1822.

Otis Tileston *d* 1837
Jacob Bancroft *t* 1825
Abigail Q. Gray *t* 1832
Ann Burchstead *t* 1836
Elizabeth Greenwood (Hovey) *t* 1841

Martha Jellison
Dorcas Butterfield *t* 1827
Eunice F. Tucker (Carlton) *t*
1826
t Newton Willey *t* 1825
t Lucretia Willey *t* 1825
t Kezia Butler *d*

September 1, 1822.
t Charles Farrar *t* 1828

December 1, 1822.

Charles W. Homer *t* 1827
Edward Burnham *e* 1834
Julius A. Palmer *t* 1825
John C. Furber *t* 1829
Anna Badger *t* 1858
Abigail Herman (Kent) *t* 1828
Eliza Andrews (Patten) *t* 1826
Susan Brown *d*
Ann B. Akerman *d* 1845
t Abby H. Thayer *t* 1830
Ruth G. Braynard *t* 1839
t Hannah Appleton *t* 1828
t Betsey Eaton *t* 1843

March 2, 1823.
t Rufus Anderson *t* 1825
Samuel Chase
t Henry Hill *t* 1837
t Laura P. Hill *t* 1837
t Susan E. Dwight *d* 1839
Edmund S. Holbrook
Mary Dodge (Stone) *t* 1848
Lydia Anthony Smith (Pardee)
t 1838
Josiah Hayden *t* 1840
Adaline Dodge (Homer) *t* 1827

June 1, 1823.

Joseph Valentine Bacon
Sarah Bacon *d*
Hannah A. Grozer *t* 1834
Mehitable Grozer (Kittredge) *t*
1827
Maria A. Grozer (Packard) *t*
1836
Catharine S. Kilton *t* 1827
Maria Creighton Odiorne (Richards) *t* 1828
Hannah Pratt (Burridge) *t* 1847

Joanna S. B. Lewis (Fernel) *t*
1828
Elizabeth Beck *t* 1835
Lydia Chapman *d*
Zebia Johnson *d* 1847
Henry John Benson *e* 1829
Bethiah Allyn *d* 1826
Alfred Grenville Benson *t* 1830
Nathaniel Trumball *t* 1823
t Dexter C. Force *d*
Amos H. Haskell *t* 1825
Joseph B. Beckford *t* 1830
Martha D. Shed (Chapin)
Charlotte Adams *d* 1823
Ray Palmer *t* 1830
Daniel N. Smith *t* 1831
Ann Cunningham *t* 1829
Elizabeth Griffin (Benson) *d*
Mary Ann Osborne *t* 1858
t Nancy Jones *t* 1851
Sarah Martin
Rebecca B. Remick *t* 1827
Mary B. Holmes *t* 1826
Heman Holmes *t* 1826
Tameyson G. Parker *t* 1833
Peter Hobart *t* 1835
Frances Pennyman (Appleton)
James Peabody *d*
Lucy Longly *t* 1835
Ann Maria Dyer
Maria Howland *t* 1827
Nancy Newman (Sumner) *t*
1841
Margaret Reed
Thompson Kidder *t* 1823
Edward Haskell *t* 1835
t Lucy Chandler *t* 1851
Lydia Patten *t* 1833
Elizabeth G. Smith (Goodnow)
t 1827
Isabella Miller (Lauren) *t* 1830
Rufus Holbrook *d* 1824
James M'Cumber *e* 1831

September 7, 1823.
t Hannah Bartlett *t* 1832
Sally Thomson
t Elizabeth Wentworth (Taylor)
t 1832
Mary Barber *t* 1832
Benjamin Judkins
Maria Jones
Charles D. Taft *e* 1829

William Beck *t* 1835
Sally Norton *t* 1826
Jeremiah Peabody *t* 1835
Catharine Peabody *t* 1835
William T. Eustis
Jacob Peabody *t* 1844
L. P. Grosvenor *t* 1825
N. P. Willis *e* 1829
Samuel G. Barnes *t* 1828
t Wealthy Ann Jenkins *t* 1852
William Tileston *e* 1828
Henry Knapp *e* 1829
Josiah F. Bumstead *t* 1827
William Henry Little *t* 1826
Eliza B. Tileston (Killem) *t* 1828
Mary Ann Gray *t* 1844
Eliza Ann Nickerson *t* 1853
Elvira Nickerson *t* 1850
Louisa H. Willis (Dwight) *d*
Lucy M. Peabody (Palmer) *t* 1828
Julia D. Willis
Lydia Starr (Vanvooris) *d*
Frances C. Ingalls (Greenough) *t* 1840
Ruth Titcomb (Spare) *t* 1837
Martha Ann F. Everett *t* 1829
Elizabeth B. Coburn *t* 1825
Adeline N. S. Fullerton *t* 1827
Marcia Grozer *t* 1835
Adeline Gleason (Sprague)
Desire Smith *t* 1835
Sarah Lambert *t* 1825
George T. Fisher *t* 1827
Thomas A. Davis *t* 1825
t Sally W. Lang
Lucy Baldwin *d* 1845

December 7, 1823.

Gloriana E. Rogers (Haskell) *t* 1826
Hannah P. Train *t* 1831
Rebecca B. Watts *t* 1826
Nancy Tileston *d* 1831
Achsah Richards *t* 1836
William J. Hubbard *t* 1827
Sophronia Abbot *t* 1847
Lucy Nutting (Kelf) *t* 1844

March, 1824.

Edmund Munroe
t Dorcas Hayden *t* 1840

Sally Bicknal
Charles Willey *t* 1826
Joseph Jenkins, Jr. *t* 1842
Rachel Frost (Green) *t* 1828
t Eunice Hale *t* 1831
Hannah Furber *t* 1836
Mary Perley (Twombly) *t* 1826
t Louis Dwight *d*
Sarah Fisk (Gallot) *t* 1840
t Daniel Colby
t Lydia Colby

June, 1824.

Eliza Pray (Hyde) *t* 1832
t Sophia Dean (Mumford) *t* 1842
t Mary Ann Dean (Hale) *t* 1829

September, 1824.

Nathaniel Daniels *d* 1833
t Eliza Hill (Anderson) *t* 1827
t Elizabeth Beath *d* 1827
William R. Lovejoy *t* 1825

December, 1824.

Luke Fernal *t* 1828
t Celia Parker *t* 1830
Caroline Furber *d* 1825

March, 1825.

t Lucy Fairbanks *d*
t Sarah Johnson *e* 1829
t Hannah Johnson *e* 1829

June, 1825.

Lois C. Farnum *d*
Sarah A. Farnum *d*
t Thomas Emerson *t* 1827
Wendell Moreno *t* 1823
t Harriet Byron Mayhew

March, 1826.

Henrietta M. Benson (Homer) *t* 1836
Mark Weare *d*
Rebecca W. Parker
Mary Barton *t* 1839

[Mr. Dwight dismissed April 10, 1826.]

June 3, 1826.

George Denny *t* 1836

3

t Sophia P. Willis *t* 1844
Mary Evarts (Greene) *t* 1837
Tirzah Hartshorn *t* 1835
Susan Tates
David Tilton *t* 1830
Deborah Dean

September, 1826.

Ellen Robbins (Hobart) *d* 1832
Ebenezer Marsh *t* 1828
Harriet B. Hunt *t* 1843
Josiah Gilman *t* 1829
Emeline Lewis (Sanborn) *d*
t Eunice Dean (Drake) *t* 1836

December, 1826.

Maria Robbins
Eunice Allen *t* 1831
t Marcus Latham *t* 1850
Abigail Robbins *d*
t Susan W. Eustis
t Polly Barker (Hardy) *t* 1834
t Edward Beecher *t* 1844

[Rev. Edward Beecher ordained
December 27, 1826.]

March 3, 1827.

Abigail Daniels (Turner)
Charlotte G. Butters *t* 1829
Agness Wasson (Talbot)
Deborah W. Vinal (Fisk) *t* 1829
Eliza Chapman *t* 1833
Louisa Blethem (Huntress)
Rebecca Hurd *d* 1836
t Catharine Walley *d* 1845
Catharine H. Walley *d* 1840

June 2, 1827.

Abigail W. Graves *t* 1828
Isaac Jackson *d*
John Fullerton *d* 1844
Margaret Beckford *t* 1830
Elizabeth Ann W. Quincy
(Wales) *t* 1847
Mary P. Willis (Jenkins) *t*
1842
Ellen Prentiss (Pierce) *t* 1840
t Sarah Shaw *t* 1832
Charlotte Scales *d*
Mary C. Palmer
Abiah Bailey *t* 1836
George Bartlett *d*
John Simpson *e* 1829

Sarah C. Beath *t* 1836
John Robinson, Jr. *t* 1827
Hannah Virgin *d*
Nathan Gallot *t* 1840
Elizabeth P. Lewis *e* 1839
Joseph G. Binney *t* 1830

September 2, 1827.

Dorcas Farrar *t* 1828
Mary Bowker *t* 1831
Mary T. Carter (Bundy) *d* 1832
Martha A. Carter (Wheeler) *t*
1835
William Peirce *t* 1840
Andrew S. March *t* 1834
Margaret Akarman *d*
Hannah M. Akarman (Sutton) *d*
Dorcas Freeman Holmes (Bige-
low) *t* 1832
William Wheeler *t* 1835
Martha Knight (Morrison)
Ezra Walker
Mary H. Haven (Eldridge) *t*
1829
Margaret Hindman (Hulst)
t William G. Ladd *t* 1847
t Margaret G. Ladd *t* 1847
Mary Gallott *t* 1831
Mary Ann Cheswill (Knight)
t 1835
t Harrison O. Fay *t* 1836

December 2, 1827.

Peter Hobart, Jr.
Mary Ann Clark (Mars) *t* 1839
Mary P. Stevens (Ainsworth)
t 1847
Fanny Winslow *d* 1857
Clarissa Leavitt (Towle) *t* 1842
Sarah Coney (Sweetser) *t* 1835
Mary Edwards *t* 1837
Hannah Dana
t Eunice R. Wise *t* 1829
Francis Bundy
Jane Harris
Hannah D. Bridges (Hum-
phreys) *t* 1832
Sarah H. Cushing *t* 1836
Edward Knight *t* 1835
Martha S. Davis (Tully) *e* 1837
Ann Wiggin
Christiana Odiorne *t* 1858
Mary C. Waite (Locke) *t* 1828

Elizabeth Hammond *d*
Mary Homer
Charlotte C. Vose *d*
Mary Bemis
Mary F. Richards (Parmenter) *d* 1832
Russell Cook *t* 1848
Michael H. Simpson
t Susanna Peirce *d*
Lucinda M. Dudley *t* 1833

March 2, 1828.

Margaret Cruft *d*
Mary Bennett *t* 1844
Samuel Joslyn
Jeremiah Pierce *d* 1833
Ebenezer B. Gale *t* 1838
Sally Gale *d*
Adeline Joslyn
Priscilla Wood *d*
Joanna Lord *t* 1830
Mehitable S. Lord *t* 1830
Harriet A. Bowker *t* 1844
Rufus L. Bruce *e* 1832
t Phebe Tibbetts (Arter)
Deborah Woods (Sanford)
Charlotte S. Denny *t* 1836
Ruth W. Crockett *t* 1831
Josiah W. Blake *d*
Hannah Shepard
Emily George
t Susan Henchman *t* 1832

June 1, 1828.

Frances E. Giddings *t* 1849
Mary C. Grimes
Hannah Hunt
Mary O. Akarman (Liscom) *t* 1836
t Hannah Pierce
Ann Dunn
t Jane Vaughan *d*
Jerusha Davenport *d*

September 1, 1828.

Philip Shaw *t* 1838
Asa W. Pollard *t* 1829
t James Leach *t* 1831
t Ann Leach *t* 1831
t Mary Cowdin (Brown) *t* 1847
Irene Wyman *t* 1834
Hannah S. Carter (Kilburn) *t* 1837

t Catharine D. Weeks (Hayden) *t* 1837
t Benjamin C. Bacon *t* 1830

December 7, 1828.

Mary Blood *t* 1832
Eleanor Crane (Guild) *t* 1838
Mary P. Richards *d*
Abigail Lord *t* 1838
Caroline Kidder (Lovejoy) *t* 1834
Nathan Hunting *t* 1840
Almira Kidder (Leach) *t* 1837
t Catharine Woods *d*
John Goodhue *d* 1848
t Mary Clark *t* 1838
Ann Critchett (Barnes)
t Martha C. Henry *t* 1835

February 28, 1829.

Elizabeth D. Dix *t* 1830
Sila Pierce *d* 1837
Lucy W. Nutting
Mary Page *t* 1839
Sally Kemp (Wilcox) *t* 1844
t Patience G. Withington (Eldred) *t* 1846
t Hannah Gregory *t* 1834
t Lowell Mason *t* 1834
t Abigail Mason *t* 1834
t David B. Spencer *t* 1831
t Aurelia T. Spencer *t* 1831
t Almira Dane *t* 1844
t Mary Stratton *t* 1845
Susan Leavitt *d*
Lydia Spaulding
Rebecca S. Dean *t* 183
t Mary Ann Hubbard
Elizabeth Crane *t* 1839

June 7, 1829.

t Elizabeth Sloan *t* 1833
Samantha Cowdin (Stafford) *d* 1844
Mary Ann Calder *t* 1832
t Zachariah Gurney *d* 1838
Miriam Kidder
t Sarah Coolidge
t Jefferson French *t* 1845
t Mary Barney *d*

September 6, 1829.

t Ashur Adams *t* 1832

28

t Amelia Adams *t* 1832
Sophia Hayden *t* 1840
t Martha Evans
Samuel W. Wilson
Edgar W. Davies *t* 1846
t Hannah Lovett

December 6, 1829.

Horatio M. Willis *t* 1844
Luther Sanderson
Abigail Sanderson
Susan W. Jones *t* 1835
Hellen Soren *t* 1844
Elizabeth French *t* 1845

March 7, 1830.

t George Gregerson *t* 1835
Martha Somes *d*
t Mary Tilton
t Nicholas Gilman *t* 1832

June 5, 1830.

t Alice C. Furber
Mary B. Akarman (Bailey)
Abigail G. Judkins *d*
t Nathan Trumbull *t* 1831
John Gilbert, Jr. *t* 1847
t Daniel T. Coit *t* 1837
Catharine Gale *t* 1838

[Rev. E. Beecher dismissed October 28, 1830.]

November, 1830.

Timothy B. Mason *t* 1832
Alma Mason *t* 1832
Louisa Thompson *t* 1838
t Relief Barnes *t* 1803
t Abigail Whitney *d*
Ann Beckford *t* 1831
Elizabeth D. Bigelow *d*
Phebe Winslow

March, 1831.

t Lucy Slade *t* 1834
Mary T. Hicks (Colby)
John Greenwood *t* 1839
Elizabeth Greenwood *t* 1839
Abigail Robbins

June, 1831.

t Olive Brown (Johnson) *t* 1835

Catharine Bruce (Nevens) 1822
t Louis Rice *t* 1835
Caroline Barrett *t* 1834
t Samuel Dana Green *t* 1836
Susan Green *t* 1836
Mary Nash Quincy (Perry) *t* 1844

September, 1831.

t I. Merrill Kimball *t* 1837
Mary Jenkins *t*
Elizabeth M'Intire (Hickford) *d*
Fanny A. Cushing *t* 1857

November 30, 1831.

Sarah Ann Peabody (Converse) *t* 1834
Sally M. Knight *t* 1833
Lucy A. Haynes *d*
Jane M. Houghton (Goldsmith) *t* 1835
Horace L. Temple *t* 1843
Adalliza Fessenden (Temple) *t* 1843
Clarissa M. E. Brackett *t* 1847
G. Wait Fletcher *t* 1832
Robert Steele *t* 1851
Martha S. Evarts (Tracy) *t* 1835
Pamelia Harrison (Dustin) *t* 1840

March 2, 1832.

Elizabeth D. Kilham (Simpson)
Jane G. L. Coit *t* 1837
Sarah Cowdin *d* 1833

June 1, 1832.

Ann Elizabeth Ripley (March) *t* 1834

[Rev. Joel H. Linsley installed December 5, 1832.]

December, 1832.

Ann Brown
t Jane Griffin *t* 1838
t Mary Shaw *t* 1838
William B. Homer *t* 1836
t Nathaniel Dana *t* 1847
t Lois W. Dana *t* 1847
Medefer Haskell *t* 1835

March 2, 1833.

Horace Parmenter *t* 1842
t Josiah F. Bumstead
t Lucy D. Bumstead
  Adeline Lincoln *t* 1845
  Martha Brown *d*
t Elizabeth Whiting *d*
t Hannah J. Knapp *d* 1842
t Abigail K. Cummings
t Mary Parks *con. dis.* 1847
t Augusta M. Follansbe *t* 1835

July, 1833.

Catharine B. Titcomb *t* 1843
t George W. Ricker
t Daniel Colby
t Lydia Colby
  Caroline Colby
  Hannah S. Colby
t Luke Brown *t* 1836
t Sophronia A. Brown *t* 1836
t Curtis Searles *t* 1836
t Abigail M. Searles *t* 1836
  George Cook
  Mary Tates *d*
t Clarina S. Blake *t* 1858

August 30, 1833.

Sarah L. Coit (Scudder) *t* 1834
Mary Ann Hubbard (Blatch-
  ford) *t* 1838
Alicia H. Blatchford (Scudder)
  t 1841
Eunice Woodward *d*
Elsey G. Crooker (Chamberlain)
Charlotte A. Nickerson *t* 1853
t Johnson Colby *t* 1836
t Elizabeth Colby *t* 1836
t James Spare *t* 1837
t Susan Gould (Graves)
t William G. Hannford
  Lucy Griffith
t Phebe H. Lansley *t* 1838
t James Leach *t* 1837
t William Lawrence *t* 1836
t Sarah D. Blood (Hobart)

December, 1833.

t Sarah Spear *t* 1836
t Christopher C. Denny *t* 1834
t Harriet P. Watson *t* 1838

t Albert Smith

February 25, 1834.

Silas Allen, Jr. *e* 1846
Silas A. Quincy *t* 1847
Eliza Townson
Ephraim Jones *d* 1839
Lucy Spotford
Charles Adams *d* 1839
Sarah Adams *d*
Mary Gregg
Lydia Steele *d*
Mary Jane King *t* 1835
t Elizabeth Watts *d* 1846
Elizabeth Chubbuck
Philo Augustus Gillett *t* 1847
Sumner Jewett *t*
t Zebediah Guild *t* 1838
t Martha Carter *t* 1837
  Lucy Goodridge *d*
  Lucy A. Wright (Stearns) *t*
    1840
t Lucy Brigham
  Jonathan M. Dodd *t* 1842
  Abigail S. Dodd *t* 1842

April 28, 1834.

Elizabeth Bell *t* 1847
t Mary Ann C. Decker *d*
Mary Adaline Hersey *t* 1836
Catharine H. Maddocks (Wil-
  liams)
Sarah C. Whittle *t* 1840
Joshua R. Shedd *t* 1841
Elizabeth M. Roberts (Olds)
  t 1837
Martha Evans *d*
Mary A Miller *e* 1837
t Eliza A. Seccomb *t* 1838
Octavia A. Bacon (Forsyth) *t*
  1844
Abigail A. Quincy
William Jones *d*
John Barns *t* 1836
t John N. Turner *t* 1844
t Sarah Gove

July, 1834.

Lucy M. Beman

October 30, 1834.

Mary O. Cook *t* 1848
Nancy Daniels *t* 1836

t Varnum J. Blood *t* 1840

t Rebecca C. Perkins (Fiske) *t* 1840

February, 1835.

t Daniel Safford *t* 1835
t Ruth H. Safford *t* 1835
t Lucy M'Allister Frye *t* 1839
t Eliza White
t Ann Eliza Stafford *t* 1835

June, 1835.

t Charles C. Ryan *d*
t George L. Stafford

[Rev. J. H. Linsley dismissed September 28, 1835.]

October, 1835.

t Samuel Neal
t Sarah A. Neal
t Mary T. Symmes *d* 1849
t Sarah Kimball (M'Collom) *t* 1842

February, 1836.

t William Learned *t* 1845

June, 1836.

t Sophia Nay *t* 1841
t Harriet N. Ayers *d* 1843

October, 1836.

Martha Sabine

January 1, 1837.

t Francis Alexander
Lucy Gray Alexander

[Rev. Silas Aiken installed March 22, 1837.]

April, 1837.

Mary E. Ellison (Dimmick) *t* 1847
t Betsy Henry *t* 18—
t Daniel Safford *t* 1842
t Ann Eliza Safford *t* 1842
S. Ingersoll Lovett *t* 1853
Frances Ellison *t* 1847

July, 1837.

t Joshua Goodale *d* 1850
t Rebecca P. Goodale *t* 1858
t Ann B. Gilbert *t* 1847

September, 1837.

Sophia W. Willis *t* 1844
Ellen M. Nickerson (White)
Joanna P. Hubbard (Gillett) *t* 1847
t Nancy D. Learned *t* 1845
Sarah Furber *t* 1841
Jane Farmer *t* 1840
Adra E. Fessenden (Bradbury) *t* 1841
Elizabeth Bell *t*
Sophia Wildes

November, 1837.

Gertrude Catherwood
Mary S. Dana *t* 1847
t Peter Hobart *con. dis.* 1850
t Silas Aiken *t* 1849
t Sophia P. Aiken *t* 1849

January, 1838.

t Abigail Fletcher
Mary Wasson
t Zenas Cushing *d*
t Elizabeth Cushing
t Amos Johnson *t* 1842
t Eunice B. Johnson *t* 1842
t Albert B. Hill *t* 1850
t Samuel Lamson *d* 1845
t Sally Lamson *d* 1840
t Sarah Lamson

March 3, 1838.

John R. Ingalls
Eliza Ingalls *d* 1840
Elizabeth Ingalls
Eliza Ann Ingalls
Anna Page (Wadsworth) *t* 1845
t Rachel Gates
t Daniel Griffin
Harriet Colburn
Mary Sowen
Sarah Chamberlain *d*
Eveline Wheeler *d*
t Ebenezer Wheelwright *t* 1847
t Sarah Wheelwright *t* 1847
Joel Whittemore *t* 1844

t Margaret Whittemore *t* 1844
Edwin Lamson

July, 1838.

Mary S. Russell
Matilda Russell (Merriam)
Mary S. Russell (Morey)
Maria V. Derby
t Mary Blood (Lakeman) *t* 1847
Lydia F. Judkins (Poole)
Sarah M. Parker (Farnsworth)
  t 1840
Isabella G. Parker (Oviatt) *t*
  1848
Nancy Woods
Elizabeth Johnson *d* 1843
t Arad Knowlton
t Sophia Knowlton

September 11, 1838.

t William H. Mussey *t* 1843
Elmira Barnes (Shedd) *t* 1841
Luther Dana
t Mary Field
t Thirza D. Goodhue *t* 1852

November 1, 1838.

t Hannah P. Lemaire *d* 1840
t Sophronia C. Goodrich (Stafford)

January 6, 1839.

t Ferdinand G. Shauffler *t* 1841
t Margaret Shauffler *t* 1841
t Rosina Shauffler *t* 1841
t Elizabeth Heilman *t* 1841
t Harriet A. Ridgway *e* 1846
t Anna Muzzey
t Angelina B. Johnson *t* 1842

May 4, 1839.

Sarah S. W. Ellis (Knight)
t Henry Howard, Jr. *t* 1845
t Mary Howard *t* 1845
Ann Luther *d* 1845

July, 1839.

Amelia L. Porter (Brown)
Elizabeth Tates
Elizabeth L. Spaulding
t Sylvia T. Buyn *d*

August 31, 1839.

Harriet D. Turner *t* 1844
t Esther Homes *d*

November 2, 1839.

Charles Stoughton *t* 1847
t Mary Cheney (Emery) *t* 1844
Albert W. Smith *t* 1851
t Roswell W. Turner *t* 1843
t Catharine Locke *t* 1851
t Elijah Smalley
t Gideon C. Lyford *t* 1854
t Hannah E. Lyford *t* 1846
t Jerome W. Tyler *t* 1842
t Mary Elizabeth Parker
t Eliza Learned (Adam) *t*
t Alfred Richardson *t* 1845
t Rebecca W. Richardson *t* 1845
t Hosea Ilsley *t* 1841
t Abigail Ilsley *t* 1841

January 4, 1840.

t Nancy Saunders (McGee) *t*
  1841
t Hannah Jewett

May 2, 1840.

Lemuel C. Clark *t* 1844
Sarah Baxter
Sarah F. Dana
t Daniel F. Jones
Tobias O. Gardner
t Abigail Millet
Mary Carlisle (Latham)
t William V. Thomson *t* 1857

June 6, 1840.

Sara W. Eldredge (Farrington)
t Marshall N. Kenny *d*
Benjamin Judkins, Jr.
Timothy W. Hoxie
John Davis
Edmund S. Munroe *t* 1840
John H. Dane *t* 1845
William T. Eustis, Jr. *t* 1846
George F. Homer *t* 1842
Frederick G. Cary
Charles W. Eustis *d* 1842
Edward H. Parker
Frances Quinn *t* 1844
Phebe W. Payson (Dana) *t*
  1847

Miranda S. Homes (Homer) *t* 1842
Harriet N. Bumstead *t* 1841
Mary E. Washburn (Nye)
Rosanna R. Temple *t* 1848
Eliza G. Boult
Paulina T. Washburn (Munroe)
Frances Jane Washburn *t* 1853
t Eliza K. Robbins
Emily Culver *t* 1853
Elizabeth G. Proctor (Blood) *t* 1847
Joanna Ryan *d*
Charity P. Woods *d* 1849
Nancy Alexander
t Andrew C. Fearing
Aldeberonto Fearing
Edward A. Washburn
t Angelina P. Eaton

July 4, 1840.

t Amos Fisher *d*
t Ann Fisher
t Mary G. Fisher
Charles B. F. Adams
Sarah Fessenden
Mary W. Dwight
Mary Bush (Spaulding) *t* 1850
Freeman J. Bumstead
Gillam Barnes *t* 1843
Ozias C. Blanchard *e* 1849
Charlotte P. Fay (Chandler) *t* 1845
Persis Lewis (Story) *t* 1842
t Emeline Goodnow
William G. Ladd, Jr. *t* 1847
t Nathaniel E. Ide *d* 184–

September 5, 1840.

t Tamer Cary *e* 1846
t Mary Cary *t* 1848
William H. Weld *t* 1857
Sarah B. Weld *t* 1857
Sarah E. Weld *t* 1857
Elizabeth S. Leach (Peach)
Sarah A. Bradley *d* 1849
Mary Quiggin (Robertson) *t* 1848

October 31, 1840.

Henry B. Wheelright

Chastine Lincoln
Stephen Jones, Jr. *d* 1849
t Almira Jenness
Susan E. Jones
Joseph Lovell *t* 1855
Lavinia Lovett *t* 1855
Mary K. Wason (Wilson)
Jane Whitmarsh
t Deborah Carlton

January 2, 1841.

George D. Munroe
Susan F. Sanderson (Green)
Charles B. Dana *t* 1847
Richard L. Saville *t* 1853
t Reuben Balcom
t Mary B. Goodwin (Dunn)
t Abner R. Campbell *t* 1841
t Eliza S. Campbell *t* 1841
t Mary Fryer

March 6, 1841.

Susan Clapp
Sarah B. Shepard (Hyde)
Eliza Whittemore
t Hannah Barker (Abbott) *t* 1841
Mary Ann Richardson *t* 1845
George L. Richardson *t* 1845
Mahala Brown (Brown) *d*
Susan E. D. Munroe (Smith) *t* 1856
Sarah Putnam *t* 1842
Sarah H. Bacon (Cadue)
Sylvester P. Gilbert *e*
t Charles Fogg *e* 1845
t Sarah H. Stevens
t Martha Thomas
t Samuel C. Titcomb *t* 1844

May 1, 1841.

Maria L. Dwight (Eustis) *t* 1846
Philenia Wilder
Charles French *d*
George H. Hill
Elizabeth B. Homer
t Samuel Goodhue *d*
Woodbury S. Dana *t* 1844
Susan Carlisle
Lucia Ann Gates *t* 1843
Laura H. Bradshaw
t Laura A. Smalley *t* 851
t Josepha Fisher

t Sarah S. Bridge *t* 1846
t Benjamin F. Abbott

July 2, 1841.

t Martha Bradshaw *t*
t Agnes Craig
t Eliza L. Carsley *t* 1857
   Mary Chamberlain
t Susan Hobart (Howard) *t* 1847
   Sarah F. Hersey *t* 1848
t Susan W. Jones
   Francis I. Pitman *t* 1842
   Ellen W. Riddle *t* 1843
t Elizabeth K. Smith
t Charles F. Stevens *d*
   Julia E. P. Willis *t* 1844

November 5, 1841.

t Mary H. Babbitt *t* 1850
t Sarah B. Bontelle *t* 1844
t Francis E. Gray *t* 1843
   Daniel L. Giddings *d*
t Mary Ann Riddle *t* 1843
t Abigail K. Whitten *t* 1843
   George W. Wilson

December 31, 1841.

   Rebecca Chandler *t* 1848
t Sarah Cushing *d*
   Martha A. Gould (Fisher)
t Mary H. Turner *t* 1848

March 4, 1842.

t Horace J. Butterfield *t* 1850
   Caroline F. Brownell *t* 1843
t Asa C. Brownell *t* 1843
t Mary Ann Eustis *e* 1845
   Susan P. Flagg (Perkins) *t* 1846
t Horace S. Taylor *t* 1845

April 29, 1842.

   Francis G. Barnes *t* 1843
   Luther J. Barnes
   James L. Bowers
   James L. Crossett *t* 1848
t Charles F. Dennett
t Eliza Ann Eastman
   Mary E. Evans
t Betsey Hardy *t* 1857
   Susan M. Hall *t* 1842
   Thomas W. Hardy *t* 1857
   Henrietta M. Judkins *t* 1857

   Josiah F. Kimball *t* 1846
   Hannah Keegan
   Temperance B. Lane
t Frederick W. Newton *t* 1852
   Daniel Nason
   Hannah Nason
   Thomas D. Quincy *t* 1858
t Elizabeth B. Robbins *t* 1843
   Francis A. Richardson *t* 1842
   Charles H. Richardson *t* 1845
   Abby W. Ryan
t Ruth B. E. Staniels
   Rebecca E. Shattuck *d*
   Margaret F. Weatherstone *t* 1847
   Mary A. Weatherstone
   Betsey Woods

July 1, 1842.

   Mary Atwood
t Esther H. F. Burnett *t*
   Harriet Bemis
t Elizabeth Carleton *t* 1857
   Maria Cary *e* 1848
   Abby P. Carsley *t* 1857
   Phineas Cary *e* 1848
   Caroline Chamberlain
   Austin Colby *e* 1842
   George Dow
   Charles S. Evans
   Mary M. Fryer *d*
   Lucretia Fryer *t* 1848
   Eliza Ann Fryer *t* 1848
   Frances S. Gilbert (Newlin) *t* 1847
   Martha D. Gregg (Tileston)
   C. A. Gregg (Stockbridge)
   Mary A. Goodrich (Fuller)
t Caroline Hunt (Eaton) *t* 1857
   Anna C. Harris *t* 1845
   Norman W. Knowlton *t* 1853
   Julia M. Kilham (Lord)
   Benjamin F. Leavens *t* 1846
   Sylvia C. Leavens *d* 1849
   Charlotte E. Langdon *t* 1849
   Ellen A. Lyford *t* 1854
   Mary H. Low *t* 1842
   Mary E. Low *t* 1842
   Elizabeth N. Lamson (Sawyer) *t* 1844
t Alexander McWhirk *t* 1845
t Matilda McWhirk *t* 1845
   Mary Elizabeth McWhirk *t* 1845

Margaret McKay *t* 1849
Thomas W. Nickerson
t Mary S. Payson *t* 1858
Susan K. Peavy (Jones)
Eliza Russell *t* 1854
Frances D. Rappell (Whitman)
   t 1857
Charles Rand *t* 1843
Sarah F. Rogers
Rebecca S. Swan (Gustin)
John Stone *t* 1848
Mary E. Stone *t* 1848
Louisa B. Sewall (Hubbard) *d*
Margaret A. Sawyer *t* 1848
Edward G. Tileston
John T. Tufts
Mary H. Virgin
t Mary R. Woodbury *t* 1848
t Mary A. Wright *t* 1850
John Woodbury *t* 1848
Samuel West

September 3, 1842.

t Frances Atherton
t Nathan Crosby *t* 1846
t Rebecca M. Crosby *t* 1846
Daniel Copeland *t* 1854
Hannah E. Copeland *t* 1854
t Mary A. Hall
Julia A. Laiten (Woodbury) *t*
   1854
t Jessie Munsey
Sophia Munroe (Cobb) *t* 1849
t George Russell *t* 1854
t Sarah L. Russell *d*
t Emory Sawyer *t* 1848
Amory Woodbury *t* 1854

November 6, 1842.

t Mehitable Clark

December 30, 1842.

t Catharine O. Bell
t Eliza Lamprey
t Betsey Seward *d* 1850

March 3, 1843.

t Clarissa Fox

May 5, 1843.

t Sarah H. Nye *t* 1845
t Mary N. G. Pike
t James W. Smith

t Eliza F. Smith
Nancy C. Wells

July 3, 1843.

Lucy Gilpatrick *t* 1849
t Margaret Stevenson *t* 1851
t Gardner Tufts *t* 1851
t Margaret Tufts *t* 1851

September 1, 1843.

t James M. Carsley *e* 1847
t James B. Clapp
t Simon D. Dyer *t* 1845

November 3, 1843.

t William H. Brown *t* 1844
Elizabeth Dutton
t Lucy Jane Smith *t*

January 6, 1844.

t James Beadles *t* 1850
t Henry L. Parsons

March 3, 1844.

t Olive Abbott (Johnson) *t* 1849
t Olive Howard *d* 1846
Susan C. Parker (Tenny) *t*
t Lucia Thompson *t* 1857
t Perry Williams *t* 1850

May 5, 1844.

t Alice Brown *t* 1848
t Eliza D. Foster (Crossett)
   1848
t Anna W. Johnson *d*
t Hannah S. Johnson
t Artemas N. Johnson
t Edward A. Studley

July 6, 1844.

t Alphonso A. Foster *t* 1858
t Eunice C. Fellows
t Austrice Fellows
t Henry Hoyt
t Elizabeth B. Hoyt
t Levi Liscom *t* 1855
t Mary O. Liscom *t* 1855
Olivia Littlefield
t Nathaniel Munroe *t* 1846
t Sarah C. Munroe *t* 1846

January 4, 1845.

John Albert Bridge *t* 1846

March 1, 1845.
t James Butler
t Ann G. Butler
  Henry T. Mygatt *t* 1848
t Abigail T. Treat *t* 1853

May 3, 1845.
t Edward Crane
t Anne B. Crane
t Timothy Farrar
  Sarah Farrar
t Sarah E. Farrar (Burke) *t* 1848
t Margaret McCulla
t Mary Ann McCulla

July 2, 1845.
t Elizabeth Williams

November 2, 1845.
  Elizabeth Bryant
t John H. Tenney
t Betsey B. Tenney

January 2, 1846.
t Sarah Jones
t Benjamin Pierce
t Sarah A. Parker

February 28, 1846.
t Francis E. Henshaw *t* 1849
  Augusta Watts (Hunt) *t* 1857

July 5, 1846.
t Mary R. Oliver
t Emeline Worcester

November, 1846.
t Mary S. Lamson

January, 1847.
t Marcus A. Latham
t Mary Prouty *t* 1857

March, 1847.
  Sarah J. Locke (Wadsworth) *t* 1848
t Sarah Putnam *t* 1850

July, 1847.
t Ezra W. Gleason *d*
t A. L. Hoyt *t* 1854
t Lucy S. Hoyt *t* 1854

November 5, 1847.
  Samuel G. Knight
  Anne S. Munroe *t* 1852

January, 1848.
t Ezra Palmer *d*
t Susan C. Palmer *d*
t Jane M. Prescott *d*
t Mary Porter
  Clarissa B. Shattuck

March 5, 1848.
  Sarah W. Hubbard *d*
t Margaret Williams *t* 1850

June, 1848.
  Hannah Balcom
  Lydia L. S. Brown *t* 1857

[Rev. Silas Aiken dismissed July 12, 1848.]

October, 1848.
t W. L. G. Hunt *t* 1857

January 5, 1849.
t Harriet J. Beadles *t* 1850
  Margaret E. Kenniston
  Sarah J. Kenniston (Morse)

[Rev. Andrew L. Stone installed January 25, 1849.]

March 3, 1849.
  Joshua W. Adams
t Charles Demond *t* 1850
  Louisa S. Munroe
  Martha T. Nickerson

May 6, 1849.
  George W. Coburn *d*
  Mary F. Fairbanks
t Fanny B. Gleason *t* 1856
  Caroline H. Gleason *t* 1856
  Caroline L. Lewis, *t* 1858
t Rebecca Park
t Jane S. Prindall *t* 1851
t Matilda F. Stone
  Ammi Smith, Jr.

July 1, 1849.
t Henry J. Bemis
  Martha H. Blodgett *d*
  Sylvia S. H. Dana
t Anna M. Gardner *d* 1850

Laura A. Goodrich
Susan B. Giddings
Sarah W. Hutchins *t* 1853
Mary Ide Homer
William C. Hubbard *t* 1856
t Hannah H. Jones *d*
Lucy A. Leavens
John P. Lovett
Henry N. Leavens
Israel E. Linsley
Mary Ann Pierce
Esther T. Priest
t Sarah A. Perkins *t* 1853
Olivia P. Studley *t* 1853
t Thomas Wilder
t Mary Wilder *d*
t Thomas S. Wright *t* 1851
t Caroline A. Wright *t* 1851
t Charles P. Whittemore *t* 1853
Abby M. Whittemore *t* 1853

November 4, 1849.

George W. Copeland
Sarah G. Huntress
t Elizabeth Jones
t Azor Maynard
t Persis Maynard
t Nancy M. Maynard
t John W. Sullivan
t Sarah L. Sheple
t Zelia R. Tappan *t*
t Henry B. Tappan *d*
t Louisa M. Tappan *d*

January 6, 1850.

George W. Eddy *t* 1858
John E. Humphrey *t* 1858
t Ann S. Kimball *t* 1844
Sarah B. Putnam
t James S. Rutledge
t Harriet N. Rutledge
Rebecca B. Whitaker *d*

March 2, 1850.

t Ann Maria Cushing
t Mark Graves *t* 1853
t Mary M. Merriam *t* 1854
t Robert L. Merriam *t* 1854
t Avery D. Putnam
Frances M. Shattuck
t Samuel K. Whipple

May 5, 1850.

t Charles L. Bartlett
John T. Bassett
t Mary Ann Bradbury
Ann Maria Cushing
Rev. J. K. Green (Missionary)
Mary Homes
t Almira King *t* 1856
t David P. King *t* 1856
t Adeline Lincoln
t Lucinda Pierce
t Charles A. Putnam
t E. L. Putnam
C. B. Shattuck *d* 1857
t Lemuel Shattuck *d* 1859

July 6, 1850.

t David Taylor, Jr.

August 31, 1850.

Mary Jane McMullen
Caroline C. Tufts *t*
t John Cordial
t Ann Caswell *t*
t Joseph W. Mason *t*
t Nancy F. Mason *t*

November 2, 1850.

t Pamelia W. Jones *t*
t Tyler Batcheller
t Abigail J. Batcheller
t Seth Goldsmith *t*
t Jane A. Goldsmith *t*

January 4, 1851.

William Allen *t*
t Mary L. Campbell
Hannah Holbrook Hosmer
Eunice Belcher
Elizabeth B. Gilbert
t Thomas F. Chase
t Elizabeth P. Chase
t Alexander Stover *t*
Augustus C. Hosmer
t John Gilbert, Jr.
t Ann B. Gilbert
t J. B. Miller
t Catharine E. Lord *t*
t Marianne M. P. Lord *t*
t D. S. Miller

March 1, 1851.

t Orin Carpenter *d*

t Abby W. Carpenter *t*
t John Tuttle
  Frances H. Wood
t Ezra Weeks
t Hannah Weeks

May 4, 1851.

  Thomas Stephenson Pycott *t*
t Samuel Gregory
t Julia A. Talcott
t Allen Litchfield *t*
t Sarah Litchfield *t*
t Mary A. Litchfield
t Mary E. Litchfield
  Franklin D. Wood
t H: G. Utford, Jr.
t William P. Towne *t*
t Eliza Holland

July 5, 1851.

Martha Parsons Trask

September 6, 1851.

t Stella L. Cleaveland
t Mary A. Winn
  Margaret Ellen Bradbury
  Joseph A. White *t*
  Jane E. White *t*
  Lucy Colburn

November 1, 1851.

t Frederic Dame
t Arabella U. G. Callender
  John Bunce

January 3, 1852.

t John R. Clute
t Betsey B. Bartlett
t Margaret S. Achorn
  George W. Plummer
t C. D. Carpenter *t*
t Wm. S. Bartlett
t Deborah Whipple
  George Foster
  Anna S. Gregg *t*
  Sarah Crocker Brewster
t Eliza T. Pierce
t Abby C. Pierce
t Charles W. Robinson
t Sarah Ann Robinson
t E. S. Chesbrough *t*
t C. A. Chesbrough *t*

March 6, 1852.

  Seymour Lyman *t*
  Calvin W. Gibbs *t*
t Job Lockwood
t Mary J. Lockwood
t Wm. Horton
t Matthew H. Merriam *t*
  Jane Wilde *t*
  Samuel W. Mason *t*
  Ephraim Morris *t*
  Thomas Hill
  Charles Mellen *t*
t Mary Robinett
  Frances A. Judkins (Bond)
  Sarah E. Judkins (Macy) *t*
  Eunice Wier
t Jeremiah Hurd
t Martha C. Hurd
t Hiram B. Allen
  Elizabeth M. Lane

May 2, 1852.

  Alfred A. Ellsworth
t J. Fullarton, Jr.
t Mary A. Fullarton
t Harriet Torry
  Sarah Eliza Chandler
t Lucius H. Briggs *t*
t Elizabeth H. Briggs *t*
  Jane T. Tedder
  Sarah Jane Spilman *t*
t Chalmer S. Dawes
t Sarah E. Dawes
t Noah Davis
t Wm. S. Anderson
t H. U. Anderson
  David T. Mansfield
  Laura S. Colby *t*
t Emmeline E. Davis

July 4, 1852.

t Erastus Smith
  Naomi Augusta Goodrich
  Dixey S. Lewis *t*
  Ellen Neally
  Sarah E. Bellows
t John F. Benton *t*
t Julia A. Benton *t*
  Edward L. Barnes *t*
  Mary Ann Boothby
  Elmira Bowers *t*

September 5, 1852.

Hannah E. Hasty (Morgan)
t Jane M. Bedford (Willcut)
Wm. Livermore *t*
Thomas Jordan *t*
Daniel H. Young
t Martha Williams *t*

November 6, 1852.

t Robert Mac Adam
Mary A. Flagg
Martha E. Clapp
Mary E. Davis
James Brown
t Porter Brown *t*
Frederic Carr *t*

January 1, 1853.

Eliza Cutter
t Joel H. Smith *t*
t John Haven, Jr.
t Emily R. Haven *d*
Joseph C. Merrill
t Annis Hodgkins (Clark)
t Nathaniel Willis
t Susan D. Willis
t Mary A. Storer *t*
t Sarah F. Maxwell
t Alexander Greer
t Margaret McConnaghy

March 5, 1853.

t Isabella Greer
Mary G. Judkins
Hannah Elizabeth Judkins
t Martha L. Travas *t*
t Oliver D. Root *t*
Ellen A. Doolittle (Cooke)
t Abigail Ross
Abby Porter
Roxanna P. Hill
t Hannah S. Cudworth
Anna L. Pomroy *t*
Mary Wallis Waldron
Cynthia White *t*
Nancy S. Knowlton
t John F. Morgan
t James W. Cudworth
John L. Doty
Jeannie Humphrey (Nickerson)
t Miranda Hill
t Mary F. Q. French

April 30, 1853.

t Harriet N. Sawyer
John W. Hilton
Eliza De Lap
t Mary J. Hooper
Mary M. Lord
Elizabeth J. Reed
t Lyman B. Ripley

July 2, 1853.

t Mary E. Preble
L. Ellen Sprague
t Wm. B. Melvin
t Mehitable Loring
t J. Hamilton Farrar *t*
t Mary A. Newton
t Mary Peake
t Pamelia D. Allen
t John J. Newcomb
t Mary S. Newcomb
Sarah A. Niblick
Isaac Parker *d*
Mary E. Case *e*
t Leonard Carsley *d*
t George W. Jameson

September 11, 1853.

t Ezra Farnsworth
t Sarah M. Farnsworth
John Thurston Judkins
Isaac Francis Dobson

November 5, 1853.

t Julia C. Bird (Doty)
t Ebenezer L. Kelsey
t Elias C. Chapin
t Francis M. Kimball
t Francis H. Williams
t Samuel A. Brackett

January 1, 1854.

t Rebecca V. Stratton *t*
t Sophia Berry
t Sarah Brady
t Hannah B. Hadley
t Wm. Cooley, Jr.
t Emily M. Cooley
t Mary A. Hitchcock
t Caroline A. C. Morey
t Martha B. Farrar

March 4, 1854.

t Abby O. White
t Mary Elizabeth Grindall t
t Adeline Holmes
George S. Barker d
Mary E. Hoxie

May 6, 1854.

t Amos P. Hawley t
t F. E. Hale t
t C. W. Hale t
t George Whipple d 1856
t Eliza V. Ray
t Margaret Topping
t Elizabeth H. Whitely
t Wingate P. Sargent t
t Calista B. McPherson
t Orfa B. McPherson
Edward L. Clark t
Susan J. Clark

June 28–30, 1854.

t Mary L. Lyman t
t S. T. Bacon
Josiah B. Hagar
t Daniel Henshaw
Mary A. Hagar

November 4, 1854.

t James Robinson
t Hepsibeth M. Robinson
t Cornelia D. J. Foster
Caroline H. Foster
t Sabra T. Burditt
James R. Burditt
t Harriet Ann Fowles t
t J. A. Howard
t Mary A. Howard
t George H. Jones

January 6, 1855.

t Mary Townsend
Edward C. Townsend
t William Miller t
t Lucena Palmer
Mary E. Hobart
S. Ellen Hobart
t Lydia Stone
t E. A. Whipple t
t Rebecca W. Miller t

March 3, 1855.

t Clarissa J. Kittredge

Angelia C. Graves
t Mary Ann Root
Calvin G. Hutchinson
t J. Maria Adams
Fitz Henry Knight t
t Owen Carr t
Mary Knight

May 4, 1855.

Julia Towle
t Lucia A. Twitchell
Anna O. Jones
Harriet N. Sargent t
Mary P. Sargent t
t Wm. F. Poole t
Fanny M. Poole t
t Eliza D. Dickinson

June 29, 1855.

t Henry D. Tyler
Elijah C. Simpson
t J. E. Haven
t Richard Tiner
John H. Robinson
Enoch E. Blake
Charles C. Litchfield
t Hannah M. Sutton d
Margaret A. Sutton
Anna S. Blake
t Mary A. Barnett t
t Nathan C. Withington t

September 2, 1855.

Edward Twitchell
Emeline Twitchell
Eliza A. Holley
t Henry A. L. French t
Emeline A. Briggs t

November 4, 1855.

t Harrison O. Briggs
t H. Elizabeth Briggs
Waldo H. Jordon
John March Tyler
t Catharine Morrison

January 4, 1856.

t Edward R. Knights
Eliza A. Goodale t

February 29, 1856.

t Wm. W. Goodwin

t Rebecca W. Richardson
t Mary Ann Richardson
Hannah Maria Sutton
t Frederick Driscoll *t*

May 2, 1856.
t John C. George
Moses Dorr
Anna L. W. Eustis (Welch) *t*
John N. Chapman
Hannah D. Chapman
t J. Edwin Briggs
t Harriette R. Briggs

July 5, 1856.
Margaret Albree
Rebecca Thompson
Sarah Emily Morton
John F. Hale
Stephen O. Thayer
t Susan F. Warren
E. M. Newcomb

September 5, 1856.
Ann Smith

October 10, 1856.
James J. Rutledge *d*

October 31, 1856.
Frances A. Poole
Martha D. Tolman
Elizabeth W. W. Eustis
t Thomas W. Guild

January 2, 1857.
t Hannah H. Haskins
Syrena Morse
Lydia A. Gordon (Thayer)

February 27, 1857.
Joseph A. Jackson
t Martha R. Taylor
Abbie Le Favor
Amos S. Taylor

May 1, 1857.
Samuel C. Leavitt
t Henry N. Tilton
Anna M. M. Tilton

t B. F. Jaquith
t Harriet A. Jaquith
Sarah Ann Powers
t Ann Floyd
Lucy A. Judkins
Lucy J. Rice
Jane R. Lull
Harriet Dunbar
Mer-ylvia Jones
Sarah S. Cooper
Edward B. Hall
Henry H. Burgess
t Henry F. Coe
t Richard W. Davenport
Francis A. Spear
Cordelia L. Eaton
Lydia G. Gardner
Harriott Bartlett
Harriott L. Bartlett

July 2, 1857.
Ann E. Kimball
Alice E. Sutton
Martha L. Miller
Louisa T. Blodgett
Joseph A. Bailey, Jr.
Caroline Palmer
Elizabeth C. Light
t Harriet E. Foxcroft
Mary M. R. Tolman
Vesuvia P. Foster *t*
Elizabeth Williams
Mary R. Farnsworth
Ezra Farnsworth, Jr.
Helen F. Barnes
Mary D. Parker
t George L. Smith
t Elizabeth R. Smith
Hannah L. Richards
Nancy Hawkins
Warren G. Comey
Mary E. Comey
Marion McAdam
Maria E. Smith
t Win. B. Shorey
Anna B. Kimball
t Andrew Allison
Amos S. Young
Julia E. N. Young
Epps Choate
Ann B. Choate
Louisa C. Richardson

George Crosby, Jr.
t Joseph H. Tucker
John R. Fairbanks
Ira Grover, Jr.
Chester F. Hardon
Frank J. Jones
Thomas F. Ellis t
Charles Hunting
t Newton R. Earle
Hannah Hilton
t Oliver B. Coe
Eben Cutler
Carrie H. Cutler
H. Victoria Rutledge
Francis E. Bundy
Adelaide L. Sears t
Emma E. Sears t

September 5, 1857.

Wm. D. Anderson t
N. W. Farley
Samuel R. Smith
Eliza A. Smith
Edward O. Ballard
Thomas E. Coxe t
Wm. H. Gerrish
t Oliver B. Lothrop
t Reuben B. Doane
Ellen M. Huntress
C. Henry Smith
t Betsey Wedge
t Harriet L. Wedge (Kendall)
t Pamelia H. Farley
t Olivia E. Forrister
t Melvina A. Forrister
t Emily A. Forrister
t Emily J. Forrister
Anna M. Curtis

October 30, 1857.

Susan E. Merriam
Melvina King t
Emma A. Temple
Harriet E. Foxcroft
Maria Plimpton
Frances L. Cushing
t H. P. Dillenback
t Regina Dillenback
t John L. Richards, Jr.
t E. Hibbard Richards
Wm. H. Hutchinson
Lizzie Whitney

John Edwin Parker
t Sarah W. Simonds
t H. N. Lincoln
Maria Turner
Frederick Wm. Batchelder
t Richard Griffiths t
t Wm. H. Hyde t
Franklin Crosby
t Mary S. Crosby
Abby T. Sanderson
Fanny W. Holmes
t Mary F. Bennett
Elizabeth M. Holmes
Susan E. Whitehouse

December 13, 1857.

M. Emma Brigham

January 1, 1858.

t Giles Pease
t M. R. Pease
Catharine K. Fowler
t Sarah Cooper
t Nancy Jane Fogg
t Jane Drinkwater
Lydia A. Small
t Benj. H. West
t Elizabeth A. West

March 5, 1858.

t William Bushnell
t Juliaette P. Bushnell
t Elizabeth Mirick
t Eliza Chapman
t Emma H. Pease
Delia F. Woods
Ellen C. Jaquith
Wm. Craig

April 30, 1858

John C. Loring
Mary Ann Dolan
Adeline Stockbridge
t Emily A. Farwell
t Rufus S. Downe
t Abby A. Downe
t Eleanor H. Silsby
Julia C. Moses
John B. Arnold
t Henry Frost
John H. Burtt
t John S. Parker

4 *

Adams Twitchell
Elbridge McAlvin
t Lydia A. McAlvin
Sarah F. Davis
t Samuel Dorr, Jr.
t Louisa E. Hale
t Charles F. Jackson
t Hannah H. Hodgdon
t Sylvester P. Hodgdon
t Samuel Hodgdon
Louisa M. Harris

July 2, 1858.

Rose B. Wilkins
Anna R. Richardson
Susan C. Glidden
Mary Blodgett
Evander O. Tozier
James W. Locke
Abby S. Vaughan
Emily A. Perkins
t Lydia A. Hanson
Helen S. Gilbert
Laura Wildes
Ellen M. Warner
Sarah B. Witham
Sarah H. Odell
t Mary H. Dawley
Jane Leathers
t Susan E. P. Brown
Emmabel S. Baily
Henrietta L. Mayo
Annie E. Underhill
Henry L. Hobart
Julia L. Cutter
t Martha O. Beath
Sarah E. Beath
Mary Ann Yerxa
Leila F. Newcomb
Charles B. Newcomb
Ellen M. Perkins
Aurelia B. Cass
Ellen L. Eaton
Asa Lewis
Cordelia M. Lewis
Martha A. Smith
Elizabeth F. Smith
Annie J. Holmes
t N. F. Kwinkelenberg
t W. Kwinkelenberg
Sarah A. Rea
H. Annie Pollock
Susan Webber

Timothy Gay
t Sarah J. Turner
Anna A. Dodge *d*
J. Warren Dodge
Charles H. Hodgdon
George Gowing
Henry C. Ray
t Horace Holmes
Erastus H. Doolittle, Jr.
Charles L. Bushnell *d*
Wm. A. Blake
Edward F. Thayer
Timothy T. Parkinson
H. A. Whitney
E. Irving Wright
Horace Bumstead
David Kwinkelenberg
Sherburne D. Hutchins
John F. McClure
Augustus A. Cass
Robert R. MacAdam
John W. Matthews
A. Otis Swain
Geo. Augustus Foxcroft, Jr.
t Rebecca Rice
t Mehitable P. Gay
Frederic H. Dodge

September 3, 1858

Mary M. Taylor
Annie G. Lord
Phebe H. West
Emma E. W. Thomas
W. A. Hunting
George A. Richards
Wm. E. Gay

November 1, 1858.

Matilda J. Griffith
t Maria J. Barnard
Henry C. Cooke
C. C. Favor
James E. Otis
Edward P. Bancroft
William A. Stevens
Mary W. Wells
Wm. H. Chapman
Caroline A. Hunting
Sarah E. Hunting
Edward H. Tower
t Ambrose ne Latchfield
t Sophia L. Waterbury

George B. Eddy
Anna DeWolfe Bartlett

December 31, 1858.

t Mary A. Smith
Delia T. Smith
t Horace Houghton
t Catharine Chandler
J. Green Jones
John H. Sanderson
t Mary Keith
t Martin L. Keith
t Elizabeth C. Jones

February 27, 1859.

t Alfred C. Garratt
t Martha C. Garratt

t Martha A. Willard
t Elizabeth P. Foss
t Ann E. C. Wainwright
t Ellen E. Palmer
t Fidelia Boswell
t Estus M. Lincoln
Laura A. Haskell
May Gertrude Ladd
Abby Gertrude Latham
Annie B. Kimball
Annie R. Morse
Susan M. Fowler
G. Sumner Mann
Franklin Allison
William W. Hill
Elizabeth F. Dix

PRESENT MEMBERS

OF

PARK STREET CHURCH,

February 27, 1859.

OFFICERS.

Rev. ANDREW L. STONE, Pastor.

DEACONS.

JOSIAH BUMSTEAD,	EZRA FARNSWORTH,
EDWIN LAMSON,	TYLER BATCHELLER,
HENRY HOYT,	CHARLES C. LITCHFIELD,

JACOB FULLARTON.

CLERK.

CHARLES C. LITCHFIELD

EXAMINING COMMITTEE.

OFFICERS OF THE CHURCH, together with four brethren annually elected.

NAMES OF MALES.

Abbott, Benjamin F.	Barnes, Luther
Adams, Charles B. F.	Bartlett, Charles L.
Adams, Joshua W.	Bartlett, Wm. S.
Alexander, Francis	Batcheller, Tyler
Allen, Hiram B.	Batchelder, Frederic Wm
Allison, Andrew	Bassett, John T.
Allison, Franklin	Bemis, Henry J.
Anderson, Wm. S.	Blake, Enoch E.
Arnold, John B.	Blake, Wm. A.
	Bowers, James L.
Bacon, Joseph V.	Brackett, Samuel A
Bacon, S. T.	Briggs, Harrison O.
Bailey, Joseph A. Jr.	Briggs, J. Edwin
Balcom, Reuben	Brown, James
Ballard, Edward O.	Bumstead, Josiah
Bancroft, Edward P.	Bumstead, Josiah F.

5

Bumstead, Horace
Bumstead, Freeman J.
Bunce, John
Bundy, Francis
Bundy, Francis E.
Barditt, James R.
Burgess, Henry H.
Burtt, John H.
Bushnell, William
Butler, James

Cary, Frederick G.
Cass, Augustus A.
Chapman, John N.
Chapman, Wm. H.
Chase, Samuel
Chase, Thomas F.
Choate, Epps
Clapp, James B.
Clark, Isaac
Coburn, George W.
Colburn, Joshua
Coe, Henry F.
Coe, Oliver B.
Colby, Daniel
Comey, Warren G.
Cook, George
Cooke, Henry C.
Cooly, Wm. Jr.
Copeland, Geo. W.
Cordial, John
Craig, Wm.
Crane, Edward
Crosby, Franklin
Crosby, George, Jr.
Cudworth, James W.
Cutler, Eben

Dame, Frederic
Dana, Luther
Davenport, Richard W.
Davis, John
Davis, Noah
Dawes, Chalmer S.
Dennet, Charles F.
Dillenback, H. P.
Doane, Reuben B.
Dobson, Isaac F.
Dodge, Frederic H.
Dodge, J. Warren
Doolittle, Erastus H. Jr.
Dorr, Moses
Dorr, Samuel Jr.

Dow, George
Doty, John L.
Downe, Rufus S.

Earle, Newton R.
Eddy, George B.
Ellsworth, Alfred A.
Eustis, Wm. T.
Evans, Charles S.

Fairbanks, John R.
Farley, N. W.
Farnsworth, Ezra
Farnsworth, Ezra, Jr.
Farrar, Timothy
Favor, Charles C.
Fearing, Andrew C.
Foster, George
Foxcroft, Geo. Augustus, Jr.
Frost, Henry
Fullarton, Jacob

Gardner, Tobias O.
Garratt, Alfred C.
Gay, Timothy
Gay, Wm. E.
George, John C.
Gerrish, Wm. H.
Gilbert, John, Jr.
Goodwin, Wm. W.
Gowing, George
Green, J. K. Rev. (Missionary)
Greer, Alexander
Gregory, Samuel
Griffin, Daniel
Grover, Ira, Jr.
Guild, Thomas W.

Hale, John F.
Hall, Edward B.
Hagar, Josiah B.
Hanaford, Wm. G.
Hardon, Chester F.
Hatch, Winsor
Haven, J. E.
Haven, John, Jr.
Henshaw, Daniel
Hill, Thomas
Hill, William W.
Hilton, John W.
Hobart, Peter, Jr.
Hobart, Henry L.
Hobbs, John S.

Hodgdon, Charles H.
Hodgdon, Samuel
Hodgdon, Sylvester P.
Holbrook, Edmund S.
Holmes, Horace
Hosmer, Augustus C.
Horton, Wm.
Houghton, Horace
Howard, J. A.
Hoxie, Timothy W.
Hoyt, Henry
Hunting, Charles H.
Hunting, Wm. A.
Hurd, Jeremiah
Hutchins, Sherburne D.
Hutchinson, Calvin G.
Hutchinson, Wm. H.

Ingalls, John R.

Jackson, Charles F.
Jackson, Joseph A.
Jameson, George W.
Jaquith, B. F.
Jenkins, Joseph W.
Johnson, A. N.
Jones, Frank J.
Jones, George H.
Jones, J. Greene
Jordan, Waldo H.
Joslyn, Samuel
Judkins, Benjamin
Judkins, Benjamin, Jr.
Judkins, John T.

Keith, Martin L.
Kelsey, Ebenezer L.
Knights, Edward R.
Knight, Samuel G.
Knowlton, Arad
Kwinkelenberg, David
Kwinkelenberg, W.

Lamson, Edwin
Latham, Marcus A.
Leavens, Henry N.
Leavitt, Samuel C.
Lewis, Asa
Lincoln, Estus M.
Linsley, Israel E.
Litchfield, Charles C.
Locke, James W.
Lockwood, Job

Loring, John C.
Lothrop, Oliver B.
Lovett, John P.

Mac Adam, Robert
Mac Adam, Robert K.
Mann, G. Sumner
Mansfield, David T.
Maynard, Azor
Mathews, John W.
McAlvin, Elbridge
McClure, John F.
Melvin, Wm. B.
Merrill, Joseph C.
Miller, Joseph K.
Moors, Isaac J.
Morgan, John F.
Munroe, Edmund
Munroe, George D.

Nason, Daniel
Neal, Samuel
Newcomb, John J.
Newcomb, Edgar M.
Newcomb, Charles B.
Nickerson, Thomas W.

Otis, James E.

Parker, Edward H.
Parker, John Edwin
Parker, John S.
Parkinson, Timothy T
Parsons, Henry L.
Pease, Giles
Pierce, Benjamin
Plummer, George W.
Putnam, Avery D.
Putnam, Charles A.

Ray, Henry C.
Richards, George A.
Richards, John L., Jr.
Ricker, George W.
Ricker, Henry
Ripley, Lyman B.
Robinson, James
Robinson, Charles W.
Robinson, John H.
Rutledge, James S.

Sanderson, Luther
Sanderson, John H.

Shorey, William B.
Simpson, Elijah C.
Simpson, Michael H.
Smalley, Elijah
Smith, Albert
Smith, Ammi, Jr.
Smith, Charles H.
Smith, Erastus
Smith, George L.
Smith, Joseph B.
Smith, Samuel R.
Spear, Francis A.
Stafford, George L.
Stevens, William A.
Strong, Woodbridge
Studley, Edward A.
Sullivan, John W.
Sunderland, Edward A.
Swain, A. Otis

Taylor, Amos S.
Taylor, David, Jr.
Tenney, John H.
Thayer, Edward F.
Thayer, Stephen H.
Thayer, Stephen O.
Tileston, Edward G.
Tilton, Henry N.
Tiner, Richard
Tower, Edward H.

Townsend, Edward C.
Tozier, Evander O.
Tucker, Joseph H.
Tufts, John T.
Tuttle, John
Twitchell, Adams
Twitchell, Edward
Tyler, Henry D.
Tyler, John Marsh

Ufford, H. G., Jr.

Walker, Ezra
Washburn, Edward A
Weeks, Ezra
West, Benjamin H.
West, Samuel
Wheelwright, Henry B.
Whipple, Samuel K.
Whitney, H. A.
Wilder, Thomas
Williams, Francis H.
Willis, Nathaniel
Wilson, George W.
Wilson, Samuel W.
Wood, Franklin D.
Wright, E. Irving

Young, Amos S.
Young, Daniel H.

NAMES OF FEMALES.

Achorn, Margaret S.
Adams, J. Maria
Albree, Margaret
Alexander, Lucia Gray
Alexander, Nancy
Allen, Pamelia D.
Anderson, Harriet N.
Appleton, Frances
Atherton, Frances
Atkins, Winifred
Atwood, Mary

Baily, Emmabel S.
Bailey, Mary B.

Baker, Mary Ann
Balcom, Hannah H.
Barnard, Maria J.
Barnes, Ann
Barnes, Helen F.
Bartlett, Betsey B.
Bartlett, Harriott
Bartlett, Harriott Louise
Bartlett, Anna DeWolfe
Batcheller, Abigail J.
Baxter, Sarah
Beath, Martha O.
Belcher, Eunice
Bell, Catharine O.

Bellows, Sarah E.
Beman, Lucy M.
Bemis, Harriet
Bemis, Mary
Bennett, Mary F.
Berry, Sophia
Bicknal, Sally
Blake, Anna S.
Blake, Clarina S.
Bliss, Martha W.
Blodgett, Mary
Blodget, Louisa T.
Boult, Eliza G.
Bond, Frances A.
Boswell, Fidelia
Bradshaw, Laura H.
Brady, Sarah
Brewster, Sarah Crocker
Briggs, Elizabeth H.
Briggs, Harriette R.
Brigham, Lucy
Brigham, M. Emma
Brown, Amelia L.
Brown, Ann
Brown, Susan E. P.
Brown, Mary
Bryant, Elizabeth
Bumstead, Lucy D.
Bumstead, Mary G.
Bundy, Ann
Burditt, Sabra T.
Bushnell, Juliaette P.
Butler, Ann G.

Caduc, Sarah H.
Callender, Arabella W. G.
Campbell, Mary L.
Carlisle, Susan
Carleton, Deborah
Cass, Aurelia B.
Catherwood, Gertrude
Chamberlain, Caroline
Chamberlain, Mary
Chamberlain, Elsey G.
Chandler, Sarah Eliza
Chapin, Martha D.
Chapman, Eliza
Chapman, Hannah D.
Chase, Elizabeth P.
Choate, Ann B.
Chubbuck, Elizabeth
Clapp, Martha E.
Clapp, Susan

Clark, Annis
Clark, Hannah E.
Clark, Melatable
Clark, Susan J.
Cleaveland, Stella L.
Colburn, Eunice
Cody, Sarah
Colburn, Harriet
Colburn, Lucy
Colby, Caroline
Colby, Hannah S.
Colby, Lydia
Colby, Mary T.
Comey, Mary E.
Cooke, Ellen Adelia
Coolidge, Sarah
Cooley, Emily M.
Cooper, Sarah
Cooper, Sarah S.
Craig, Agnes
Crane, Anna B.
Crosby, Mary S.
Cudworth, Hannah S.
Cummings, Abigail K.
Curtis, Anna M.
Cushing, Ann Maria
Cushing, Ann M.
Cushing, Elizabeth
Cushing, Frances L.
Cushman, Sally
Cutler, Carrie H.
Cutler, Eliza
Cutler, Julia L.

Dana, Hannah
Dana, Sarah F.
Dana, Sylvia S. H.
Davis, Emmeline E.
Davis, Mary E.
Davis, Sarah F.
Dawes, Sarah E.
Dawley, Mary H.
Dean, Deborah
DeLap, Eliza
Derby, Maria V.
Dillenback, Regina
Dix, Elizabeth F.
Dolan, Mary Ann
Dorr, Sarah Jane
Doty, Julia C.
Downe, Abby A.
Drinkwater, Jane
Dunbar, Harriet

Dunbar, Sophia
Dunn, Ann
Dunn, Ellen
Dunn, Mary B.
Dutton, Elizabeth
Dwight, Mary Willis
Dyer, Ann Maria

Eastman, Eliza Ann
Eaton, Angelina P.
Eaton, Cordelia L.
Eaton, Ellen L.
Eustis, Elizabeth W. W.
Eustis, Susan W.
Evans, Martha
Evans, Mary E.

Farley, Pamelia H.
Farnum, Sarah A.
Farnsworth, Sarah M.
Farnsworth, Mary R.
Farrar, Martha B.
Farrar, Sarah
Farrington, Sarah W.
Farwell, Emily A.
Fearing, Aldeberonto
Fellows, Austrice
Fellows, Eunice C.
Fessenden, Sarah
Field, Mary
Fisher, Ann
Fisher, Josepha
Fisher, Mary G.
Fisher, Martha A.
Flagg, Mary A.
Fletcher, Abigail
Floyd, Ann
Fogg, Nancy Jane
Forrister, Emily A.
Forrister, Emily J.
Forrister, Melvina A.
Forrister, Olivia E.
Foss, Elizabeth P.
Foster, Cornelia D. J.
Fowler, Catharine K.
Fowler, Susan M.
Fox, Clarissa
Foxcroft, Harriet F.
Foxcroft, Harriet E.
French, Mary F. Q.
Fryer, Mary
Fullarton, Mary A.
Fuller, Mary A. G.

Furber, Alice C.

Gardner, Lydia G.
Garratt, Martha C.
Gates, Rachel
Gay, Mehitable P.
Gemmil, Dorcas
George, Emily
Giddings, Susan B.
Gilbert, Ann B.
Gilbert, Elizabeth B.
Gilbert, Helen S.
Glidden, Susan C.
Goodale, Eliza A.
Goodenow, Emeline
Goodrich, N. Augusta
Gove Sarah
Graves, Susan
Graves, Angelia C.
Gregg, Mary
Green, Susan F.
Green, Mary E.
Greer, Isabella
Griffith, Lucy
Griffith, Matilda J.
Grimes, Mary C.
Gurney, Mary L.
Gustin, Rebecca S.

Hadley, Hannah B.
Hagar, Mary A.
Hale, Louise E.
Hall, Mary A.
Hammond, Mary
Hanson, Lydia A.
Hanson, Hannah C.
Harris, Jane
Harris, Louisa M.
Haskell, Laura A.
Haskins, Hannah H.
Hawkins, Nancy
Hewins, Anna
Hill, Miranda
Hilton, Hannah
Hitchcock, Mary A.
Hobart, Mary E.
Hobart, Sarah D.
Hobart, Sarah Ellen
Hodgdon, Hannah H.
Holland, Eliza
Holley, Eliza A.
Holmes, Adeline
Holmes, Annie J.

Holmes, Elizabeth M.
Holmes, Fanny W.
Homer, Elizabeth B.
Homer, Mary
Homer, Mary I.
Homes, Isabella
Hooper, Mary J.
Hosmer, Hannah H.
Hovey, Elizabeth
Howard, Mary Ann
Hoxie, Mary E.
Hoyt, Elizabeth B.
Hubbard, Mary A.
Hulst, Margaret
Hunt, Hannah
Hunting, Sarah E.
Hunting, Caroline A.
Huntress, Ellen M.
Huntress, Louisa
Huntress, Sarah G.
Hurd, Martha C.
Hutchinson, Roxanna
Hyde, Sarah B.

Ingalls, Eliza
Ingalls, Eliza Ann
Jaquith, Ellen C.
Jaquith, Harriet A.
Jellison, Martha
Jenkins, Abigail
Jenkins, Mary
Jenness, Almira
Jewett, Hannah
Johnson, Caroline
Johnson, Hannah S.
Jones, Anna O.
Jones, Elizabeth
Jones, Elizabeth C.
Jones, Lydia
Jones, Maria
Jones, Mersylvia
Jones, Sarah
Jones, Susan E.
Jones, Susan K.
Jones, Susan W.
Joslyn, Adeline
Judkins, Hannah E.
Judkins, Lucy A.
Judkins, Mary G.

Keegan, Hannah
Keith, Mary
Kelly, Temperance B.

Kendall, Harriet L.
Kenneston, Margaret E.
Kidder, Miriam
Killiam, Priscilla
Kimball, Anna B.
Kimball, Annie B.
Kimball, Annie E.
Kimball, Frances Maria
Kittredge, Clarissa J.
Knight, Mary
Knight, Mary Ann
Knight, Sarah S. W.
Knowlton, Nancy S.
Knowlton, Sophia
Kwinkelenburg, N. F.

Ladd, May Gertrude
Lamprey, Eliza
Lamson, Mary S.
Lamson, Sarah
Lang, Sally W.
Latham, Abby Gertrude
Latham, Mary
Lawton, H. Annie
Leathers, Jane
Leavens, Lucy Ann
Leavens, Sylvia
Leavitt, Sarah
Leland, Mary F.
LeFavor, Abby
Lewis, Cordelia M.
Light, Elizabeth C.
Lincoln, Adeline
Lincoln, Chastine
Lincoln, Harriet N.
Lincoln, Sarah W.
Litchfield, Ambroscene G.
Litchfield, Mercy A.
Littlefield, Olivia
Lockwood, Mary J.
Lord, Annie G.
Lord, Julia M.
Lord, Mary M.
Loring, Mehitable
Lovett, Hannah
Lovett, Susan
Lull, Jane R.
Lyman, Margaret E.

March, Florinda J.
Martin, Sarah
Mayhew, Harriet B.
Maynard, Nancy M.

Maynard, Persis
Mayo, Henrietta L.
Maxwell, Sarah F.
MacAdam, Henrietta
M'Adam, Marion
McAlvin, Lydia A.
M'Connaghy, Margaret
M'Mullen, Mary Jane
M'Pherson, Calista B.
M'Pherson, Orfa B.
Merriam, Matilda
Mirick, Elizabeth
Millet, Abigail
Miller, D. S.
Miller, Martha L.
Morey, Caroline A. C.
Morey, Mary S.
Morgan, Hannah E.
Moors, Naamah
Morrison, Catharine
Morrison, Elizabeth M.
Morrison, Martha
Morse, Annie R.
Morse, Sarah J.
Morse, Syrena
Morton, Sarah
Morton, Sarah E.
Moses, Julia C.
Munroe, Louisa S.
Munroe, Paulina T.
Munroe, Sophia
Munsey, Jessie
Muzzy, Anna

Nason, Hannah
Neal, Sarah A.
Newcomb, Mary S.
Newcomb, Leila F.
Newhall, Sally
Newton, Mary A.
Nickerson, Jeannie
Nickerson, Martha T.
Nutting, Lucy W.
Nye, Mary E.

Odell, Sarah A.
Odiorne, Christiana
O'Harra, Eliza
Oliver, Mary R.
Orne, Caroline
Osgood, Wealthy Ann

Palmer, Caroline

Palmer, Ellen E.
Palmer, Lucena
Park, Rebecca
Parker, Mary D.
Parker, Mary Elizabeth
Parker, Rebecca W.
Peach, E. S.
Peake, Mary
Pease, Emma H.
Pease, M. R.
Peirce, Eliza T.
Peirce, Abby C.
Pierce, Lucinda
Pierce, Mary Ann
Perkins, Ellen M.
Perkins, Emily A.
Pike, Mary N. G.
Plimpton, Maria
Poole, Lydia F.
Poole, Frances A.
Porter, Abby
Porter, Mary
Powers, Sarah Anna
Pratt, Elizabeth H.
Preble, Mary E.
Priest, Esther F.
Putnam, Eunice L.
Putnam, Sarah B.

Quincy, Abigail A.
Quincy, Martha A.

Ray, Eliza V.
Ray, Mary L.
Rea, Sarah A.
Reed, Elizabeth J.
Reed, Margaret
Rice, Lucy J.
Rice, Rebecca
Richards, E. Hibbard
Richards, Hannah L.
Richardson, Anna R.
Richardson, Louisa C.
Richardson, Mary Ann
Richardson, Rebecca W.
Robbins, Abigail
Robbins, Maria
Robinette, Mary
Robinson, Hepsibeth M.
Robinson, Sarah Ann
Rogers, Sarah F.
Ross, Abigail
Russell, Mary S.

Rutledge, Harriet N.
Rutledge, H. Victoria
Ryan, Abby W.

Sabine, Martha
Sanderson, Abigail
Sanderson, Abby T.
Sanford, Deborah
Sawyer, Harriet N.
Sawyer, Susan E.
Shepard, Hannah
Sheple, Sarah L.
Shorey, Elizabeth
Silsby, Eleanor H.
Simonds, Sarah W.
Simpson, Elizabeth D.
Small, Lydia A.
Smith, Ann
Smith, Annie
Smith, Delia T.
Smith, Elizabeth F.
Smith, Eliza A.
Smith, Elizabeth K.
Smith, Elizabeth R.
Smith, Maria E.
Smith, Martha A.
Smith, Mary A.
Smith, Sarah E.
Smith, Sally W.
Smith, Vesuvia P.
Sowen, Mary
Spaulding, Elizabeth L.
Spaulding, Lydia
Spofford, Lucy
Sprague, Adeline
Sprague, Caroline H.
Sprague, Lydia Ellen
Staniels, Ruth B. E.
Stetson, Ellen (Missionary)
Stevens, Sarah H.
Stockbridge, Adeline
Stockbridge, Caroline A.
Stone, Lydia
Stone, Matilda F.
Studley, Laura A.
Sutton, Alice E.
Sutton, Hannah Maria
Sutton, Margaret A.

Talbot, Agnes
Talcott, Julia A.
Taylor, Martha R.
Taylor, Mary M.

Tedder, Jane T.
Temple, Emma A.
Tenney, Betsey B.
Thayer, Lillie A.
Thomas, Emma E. W.
Thomas, Martha
Thompson, Rebecca
Thompson, Sally
Tileston, Martha D.
Tilton, Annie M.
Tilton, Mary
Tolman, Martha D.
Topping, Margaret
Torrey, Harriet
Towle, Julia
Townsend, Mary
Townson, Eliza
Trask, Martha Parsons
Turner, Abigail
Turner, Maria
Turner, Sarah J.
Twitchell, Emeline
Twitchell, Lucia A.

Underhill, Annie E.

Vaughan, Abby S.
Virgin, Hannah
Virgin, Mary H.
Vose, Sarah

Wainwright, Ann E. C.
Waldron, Mary Wallis
Warner, Ellen M.
Warren, Susan F.
Wason, Mary
Waterbury, Sophia L.
Weatherston, Mary A
Webber, Susan
Wedge, Betsey
Weeks, Hannah
Wells, Mary W.
Wells, Nancy C.
West, Elizabeth A.
West, Phebe H.
Weston, Deborah
Whipple, Deborah
White, Abby O.
White, Eliza
White, Ellen M.
Whitely, Elizabeth H.
Whitehouse, Susan E.
Whitmarsh, Jane

Whitney, Elizabeth J.
Whitney, Lizzie
Whittemore, Eliza
Wiggin, Ann
Wier, Eunice
Willard, Martha A.
Wilder, Philena
Wildes, Laura
Wildes, Sophia
Wilkins, Rose B.
Willcut, Jane M.
Williams, Catharine H.
Williams, Elizabeth
Williams, Elizabeth

Willis, Julia D.
Willis, Susan D.
Wilson, Mary K.
Winn, Mary A.
Winslow, Phebe
Witham, Sarah B.
Wood, Frances H.
Woods, Betsey
Woods, Delia F.
Woods, Nancy
Worcester, Emeline

Yerxa, Mary Ann
Young, Julia E. N.

SUMMARY.

The whole number of persons who have been received into the Church is 1,952; — 832 by recommendation; 1,120 by profession; 675 males; 1,277 females; 255 are dead; 811 have been dismissed to other Churches; 37 excommunicated, and 2 connection dissolved. The present number (February 27, 1859) is 817, of whom 283 are males, and 564 females.

The admissions at different periods are as follows: —

At the organization, ...	26
Before Dr. Griffin's settlement, ...	18
During Dr. Griffin's ministry (3 years 9 months), .	93
In the interval (2 years 4 months), ...	44
During Mr. Dwight's ministry (8 years 6 months), .	321
In the interval (8 months), ...	20
During Mr. Beecher's ministry (3 years 10 months), .	173
In the interval (2 years), ...	39
During Mr. Linsley's ministry (2 years 10 months), .	99
In the interval (1 year 6 months), ...	10
During Mr. Aiken's ministry (11 years 4 months), .	425
In the interval (6 months), ...	3
Since Mr. Stone's settlement (10 years), . .	681
	1,952

Boston, February 27, 1859.

THE

ARTICLES OF FAITH,

AND THE

COVENANT,

OF

PARK STREET CHURCH,

BOSTON:

WITH A

LIST OF THE MEMBERS.

BOSTON:
ROCKWELL & ROLLINS, PRINTERS,
1867.

HISTORICAL SKETCH

OF

PARK STREET CHURCH.

EARLY in the year 1808, a little band of brethren of the Old South Church in this city, moved by the low estate of religion about them, the long absence of revivals, and the prevalence of doctrinal errors, formed themselves into a Society for mutual religious improvement. In the summer of the same year, encouraged and strengthened by the labors of the Rev. Dr. Kollock, of Savannah, Georgia, then on a visit to Boston, they conceived the thought of building a new house of worship and forming a new Church and Society on Evangelical principles. Having received from Dr. Kollock an assurance that if they should carry their purpose into execution, he would become their pastor, a subscription was immediately opened for the erection of a place for public worship. In a short time, through great exertions and sacrifices, they had $40,000 pledged for their work, and on the evening of February 6, 1809, a meeting of the subscribers was held to take the necessary steps in forming the new organization. A committee was appointed to draw up ARTICLES OF FAITH, and a CHURCH COVENANT; to fix upon a lot of land; and to procure the plan of a building.

The Articles of Faith and the Church Covenant were adopted February 23, 1809. On the 27th of the same month, the Council to organize the Church met at the house of William Thurston, on Beacon Hill. The churches represented were, —

The Church in Charlestown, Rev. Dr. MORSE.
The Church in Cambridge, Rev. Dr. HOLMES.
The Church in Dorchester, Rev. Mr. CODMAN.

The exercises of the occasion were as follows : — Prayer by Rev. Dr. Morse ; the reading of the 4th chapter of the Acts of the Apostles, and discourse by Rev. Dr. Morse from Psalm cxviii. 25. The Articles of Faith and Government were read by the scribe, and signed, in the presence of the Council, by nine brethren and twelve sisters. They were then declared duly organized, and Rev. Mr. Codman presented to them the fellowship of the Churches. The same evening, before the Council dissolved, five members were added by profession to the new fraternity.

A call was immediately extended to Rev. Dr. Kollock to become their Pastor, and to Rev. Dr. Griffin, then professor elect at Andover, to officiate once on each Sabbath. Dr. Griffin at once accepted the invitation, though he did not commence his public labors with them till the completion of their house.

The corner-stone of the church edifice was laid on the 1st of May, 1809, with the following inscription, —

JESUS CHRIST
THE CHIEF CORNER-STONE :
IN WHOM
ALL THE BUILDING
FITLY FRAMED TOGETHER
GROWETH
UNTO AN HOLY TEMPLE
IN THE LORD.
THIS CHURCH FORMED
FEBRUARY 27TH,
AND THIS FOUNDATION LAID
MAY 1ST, 1809.

The ceremonies were conducted by Rev. Drs. Morse and Holmes. In September, Dr. Kollock declined their call, so great was the opposition to his removing from Savannah. Dr. Griffin was then invited to become their pastor, but declined. Many other calls were given and declined. In the mean time the house of worship was completed at a cost of over $70,000, and dedicated January 10, 1810. The sermon was preached by Dr. Griffin from 2 Chronicles vi. 18.

The call to Dr. Griffin was renewed February 1, 1811, and accepted, and on the 31st of July he was installed. Dr. Griffin's ministry continued three years and nine months. He was succeeded by Rev. Sereno E. Dwight, who was ordained September 3, 1817, and dismissed April 10, 1826, after a ministry of eight years and five months. Rev. Edward Beecher was ordained as pastor in December of the same year, and exercised his ministry three years and ten months. After an interval of two years, Rev. Joel H. Linsley was installed December 5, 1832, and remained in office two years and ten months. After eighteen months, Rev. Silas Aiken was installed March 22, 1837, and dismissed July 12, 1848. Rev. Andrew L. Stone was installed January 25, 1849, and dismissed January 25, 1866. The accessions to the Church from time to time, with the duration of the pastoral office in each case, are indicated in the table at the close of the list of members.

From the beginning, 1,952 members have subscribed the covenant of this Church, of whom 853 are now with us, 255 so far as our records show, have fallen asleep, and more than 800 have gone out from us to serve the cause of Christ in other walks of Christian labor.

The first general and powerful revival of religion in the history of this Church occurred in 1823, and added to its membership about 90 converts. Another outpouring of the Spirit followed in 1826-7, which resulted in the addition to the Church of 100 members. In 1831-2, the Church was again largely blessed and increased. In the three years commencing with 1840, a powerful work of grace was enjoyed, which brought to the Church an accession of 250 members.

The connection of this Church with the movements of modern Christian benevolence is worthy of being held in grateful remembrance. The cause of Foreign Missions has been especially dear to it. The American Board, since its organization in 1810, has continued to receive the contributions of this Church. Some of the most efficient officers and members of the Board have been furnished by this Church. The Foreign Mission Society of Boston was formed in 1811, in the house of a member of this Church. The first foreign mission press furnished to the Board was projected by a member of this Church, and one fourth of its cost was given here. Since the formation of the American Board, about 180 of its missionaries have received in this house their parting instructions and farewell salutations. Here, on the 15th of October, 1819, a little band of seventeen were formed into a Mission Church to evangelize the Sandwich Islands, and the success of the enterprise is the brightest page of modern missions. For nearly fifty years there has existed in this Church a society of ladies to assist in clothing indigent pious young men while pursuing their studies for the ministry. The value of these contributions forms an aggregate of more than $10,000. In 1826 a movement was set on foot by a member of this Church, who devoted his life to the work, to improve our system of prison discipline, and ameliorate the condition of the convicts of the land. In the same year an idea was suggested and discussed at the house of one of the members of this Church, which led soon after to the formation in the city of New York of the American Home Missionary Society. The agency exerted by this Church in establishing in its present form the Monthly Concert of Prayer for the conversion of the world, in commending to general observance the annual concert of prayer for the Colleges of the land, in promoting the organization of the American Temperance Society, and the American Education Society, are matters in its history worthy of grateful commemoration. In view of such a record the Church may well exclaim, " Ebenezer," — " Hitherto hath the Lord helped us."

PASTORS.

Rev. EDWARD D. GRIFFIN, inst. July 31, 1811, dismissed April 17, 1815.
Rev. SERENO E. DWIGHT, ord. Sept. 3, 1817, dismissed April 10, 1826.
Rev. EDWARD BEECHER, ord. Dec. 27, 1826, dismissed Oct. 28, 1830.
Rev. JOEL H. LINSLEY, inst. Dec. 5, 1832, dismissed Sept. 28, 1835.
Rev. SILAS AIKEN, installed March 22, 1837, dismissed July 12, 1848.
Rev. ANDREW L. STONE, installed Jan. 25, 1849, dismissed Jan. 25, 1866.

DEACONS.

JOHN E. TYLER, chosen December 8, 1809, died January 26, 1821.
JOSIAH BUMSTEAD, chosen December 8, 1809, died Sept. 2, 1859.
JEREMIAH EVARTS, chosen May 4, 1819, died May 10, 1831.
JOHN C. PROCTOR, chosen May 4, 1819, resigned August 24, 1827.
HENRY HILL, chosen March 2, 1825, resigned April 21, 1837.
NATHANIEL WILLIS, chosen September 19, 1827, resigned Sept. 3, 1847.
NATHANIEL DANA, chosen May 14, 1835, resigned February 5, 1847.

8

DANIEL SAFFORD, chosen June 14, 1837, resigned May 27, 1842.
EDWIN LAMSON, chosen July 12, 1842.
GEORGE RUSSELL, chosen March 10, 1847, died March, 1857.
HENRY HOYT, chosen April 28, 1847.
EZRA FARNSWORTH, chosen December 14, 1853.
TYLER BATCHELLER, chosen September 17, 1857, died October 8, 1862.
JACOB FULLARTON, Jr., chosen October 13, 1857.
CHARLES C. LITCHFIELD, chosen October 13, 1857.

RULES AND REGULATIONS.

1. The weekly prayer-meetings of the Church shall be held on Friday evenings; and every such meeting shall be considered a regular Church meeting for the transaction of business.

2. The annual meeting of the Church for devotional exercises shall be held on the last Friday evening of February, except when that interferes with the preparatory lecture, in which case it shall be on the following Friday evening.

3. The annual business meeting of the Church shall be on the last Monday evening of February.

4. The Sacrament of the Lord's Supper shall be observed once in two months, namely, on the first Sabbath of January, March, May, July, September, and November, after the public services of the afternoon.

5. The preparatory lecture shall be on the preceding Friday evening.

6. The Examining Committee shall satisfy themselves of the proper qualifications of all candidates coming *either with or without certificates.*

7. Persons approved by the Committee shall be announced to the Church on Friday evening three weeks before the preparatory lecture, at which time all certificates shall be read.

8. They who are to be received from the world shall be propounded before the congregation on the second Sabbath preceding the Sacrament.

9. On the evening of the preparatory lecture the Church shall be led to a vote on the question of receiving the candidates, on condition that they shall afterwards subscribe the articles of the Church, and if they have not brought certificates, give their public assent to the covenant. The vote shall be taken on each case separately.

10. On the Sacramental Sabbath, before the administration of the ordinance, the covenant shall be read in the presence of the congregation to those who are to be received from the world, to which they shall signify their assent. At the same time the minister shall declare publicly that A, B, and C have been received by certificate from other churches, naming the churches particularly.

11. A general invitation shall be given from the pulpit previous to the Sacrament, to all members of evangelical churches present, in regular standing and full communion, to partake of the ordinance.

12. All members, absenting themselves from the worship and communion of this Church for one year or more, shall satisfy the Committee in respect to their reasons for so doing, or apply for a letter to some other church.

13. All requests for letters of dismission and recommendation shall be read at the Church meeting on Friday evening, and referred to the Examining Committee, and on the next succeeding Friday evening shall be acted on by the Church. Such letters sha'l be considered valid one year only from their date.

14. The chairmen of committees on collections shall

present in each case written reports of the sums collected, which shall be placed on the files of the Church.

15. The Clerk of the Church shall present a report, at the annual devotional meeting of the Church, of the amount of collections for benevolent purposes during the year.

16. Members of other churches, having communed with this Church for the space of one year, will be required at the expiration of that time to apply for admission, or assign to the pastor a satisfactory reason for not doing so.

17. Every candidate for the pastoral office in this Church shall be required, prior to his installation, to subscribe to the Articles of Faith adopted, by the Church, and as soon thereafter as convenient become a member of the Church.

The following table presents a list of the benevolent causes to which the Church regularly contributes, and the time of their annual presentation.

JANUARY, . .	Foreign Missions.
FEBRUARY . .	Education Society.
MARCH, . . .	American and Foreign Christian Union.
APRIL, . . .	City Missions.
MAY, ...	Bible Society.
JUNE, ...	Western College Society.
JULY, ...	Sabbath Schools.
SEPTEMBER, .	Seamen's Friend Society.
OCTOBER, . .	Home Missions.
NOVEMBER, .	Tract Society.
DECEMBER, .	Church Charities.

ARTICLES OF FAITH AND GOVERNMENT.

Adopted February 23, 1809.

WE, the Subscribers, having agreed to unite in the establishment of a new Congregational Church in Boston, by the name of *Park Street Church*, think it proper to make a declaration of that Faith which is the bond of our ecclesiastical union, and which we shall expect to find in all those who shall hereafter participate in our religious privileges and communion.

First. We believe that the Scriptures of the Old and New Testament are the Word of GOD, and the only perfect rule of Christian faith and practice.

Second. We profess our decided attachment to that system of the Christian religion which is distinguishingly denominated *Evangelical;* more particularly to those doctrines, which, in a proper sense, are styled the Doctrines of Grace, namely:

11

"That there is one and but one living, and true GOD, subsisting in three persons, the FATHER, the SON, and the HOLY GHOST; and that these Three are the one GOD, the same in substance, equal in power and glory; that GOD from all eternity, according to the counsel of His own will, and for His own glory, foreordained whatsoever comes to pass; that GOD in His most holy, wise, and powerful providence preserves and governs all his creatures and all their actions; that by the Fall, all mankind lost communion with GOD, are under His wrath and curse, and liable to all the miseries of this life, to death itself, and to the pains of hell forever; that GOD, out of His mere good pleasure, and from all eternity elected some to everlasting life, entered into a covenant of grace, to deliver them from a state of sin and misery, and introduce them into a state of salvation by a Redeemer; that this Redeemer is the Lord JESUS CHRIST, the eternal Son of GOD, who became man, and continues to be GOD and man in two distinct natures and one person forever; that the effectual calling of sinners is the work of GOD'S Spirit; that their justification is only for the sake of

CHRIST'S righteousness by faith." And though we deem no man or body of men infallible, yet we believe that those divines that were eminently distinguished in the time of the Reformation possessed the spirit, and maintained in great purity the peculiar doctrines, of our holy religion; and that these doctrines are, in general, clearly and happily expressed in the Westminster Assembly's Shorter Catechism, and in the Confession of Faith owned and consented unto by the Elders and Messengers of the Churches, assembled at Boston (N. E.), May 12th, A. D. 1680.

Third. In regard to our ecclesiastical government and discipline, with our sister churches in this Commonwealth we adopt the Congregational form, as contained in the Platform of Church Discipline, gathered out of the Word of God, and agreed upon by the Elders and Messengers of the Churches, assembled in the Synod at Cambridge (N. E.), A. D. 1648.

Fourth. In order to admission to membership in this Church, it is understood that every Candidate shall be previously examined, and give credible evidence of a ground of the comfortable hope of a par-

2

sonal condition of grace, through the renovation of the soul, by the special influences
of the HOLY SPIRIT, implying repentance
for sin and faith in JESUS CHRIST the
Redeemer.

Finally. We hereby covenant and engage, as fellow Christians of one faith, and
partakers of the same hope and joy, to
give up ourselves unto the Lord, for the
observing the ordinances of CHRIST together in the same society, and to unite
together into one body for the public
worship of GOD, and the mutual edification
one of another in the fellowship of the
Lord Jesus; exhorting, reproving, comforting, and watching over each other, for
mutual edification; — looking for that
blessed hope and the glorious appearing
of the great GOD, even our Saviour JESUS
CHRIST, who gave Himself for us that He
might redeem us from all iniquity, and
purify unto Himself a peculiar people
zealous of good works.

FORM OF ADMISSION.

You have presented yourselves in this public manner before GOD, to dedicate yourselves to His service, and to incorporate yourselves with His visible people. You are about to profess supreme love to Him, sincere contrition for all your sins, and faith unfeigned in the Lord JESUS CHRIST: to enter into a solemn covenant to receive the FATHER, SON, and HOLY GHOST, as they are offered in the Gospel, and to walk in all the commandments and ordinances of the Lord blameless. We trust you have well considered the nature of these professions and engagements. The transaction is solemn, and will be attended with eternal consequences. GOD and holy angels are witnesses. Your vows will be recorded in heaven, to be exhibited

15

on your trial at the Last Day. Yet be not overwhelmed. In the name of CHRIST you may come boldly to the GOD of grace, and provided only you have sincere desires to be His, may venture thus unalterably to commit yourselves, and trust in Him for strength to perform your vows.

Attend now to the

COVENANT.

In the presence of GOD, His holy angels, and this assembly, you do now solemnly dedicate yourselves to GOD the FATHER as your chief good; to the SON of GOD as your Mediator and Head, humbly relying on Him as your Prophet, Priest, and King; and to the HOLY SPIRIT as your Sanctifier, Comforter, and Guide. To this one GOD, FATHER, SON, and HOLY GHOST, you do heartily give up yourselves in an everlasting covenant to love and obey Him.

Having subscribed the *Articles of Faith and Government* adopted by this Church, you promise to walk with us in conformity to them, in submission to all the orders of the Gospel, and in attendance on all its ordinances, and that, by the aid of the

Divine Spirit, you will adorn your profession by a holy and blameless life.

This, you severally profess and engage.

[If the candidate have not been baptized, the Ordinance of Baptism is to be here administered.]

In consequence of these professions and promises, we affectionately receive you as members of this Church, and in the name of CHRIST declare you entitled to all its visible privileges. We welcome you to this fellowship with us in the blessings of the Gospel, and on our part engage to watch over you, and seek your edification, as long as you shall continue among us. Should you have occasion to remove, it will be your duty to seek, and ours to grant, a recommendation to another church; for hereafter you can never withdraw from the watch and communion of the saints, without a breach of covenant.

And now, beloved in the Lord, let it be impressed on your minds, that you have entered into solemn circumstances from which you can never escape. Wherever you go, these vows will be upon you. They will follow you to the bar of GOD,

2*

and in whatever world you may be fixed,
will abide upon you to eternity. You can
never again be as you have been. You
have unalterably committed yourselves,
and henceforth you *must* be the servants
of GOD. Hereafter the eyes of the world
will be upon you; and as you demean
yourselves, so religion will be honored or
disgraced. If you walk worthy of your
profession, you will be a credit and a
comfort to us; but if it be otherwise, you
will be to us a grief of heart and a vexation. And if there is a woe pronounced
on him who offends *one* of CHRIST'S little
ones, woe, woe to the person who offends *a
whole Church!* "But beloved, we are
persuaded better things of you, and things
that accompany salvation, though we thus
speak." May the Lord guide and preserve you till death, and at last receive
you and us to that blessed world where
our love and joy shall be forever perfect.
AMEN.